Love Me Merrily

ALYSSA JARRETT

 Geek Chic Press LLC

also by alyssa jarrett

The Glam Fam series

Love Apptually

Love on the Rocks

Love and Paklava

Love Me Merrily

Editing by Kristen Tate at the Blue Garret

Cover design by Nick Jarrett

ISBN: 978-1-963875-06-5 (Ebook)

ISBN: 978-1-963875-07-2 (Paperback)

Published by Geek Chic Press LLC

PO Box 1193

Oakland, CA 94604

 Formatted with Vellum

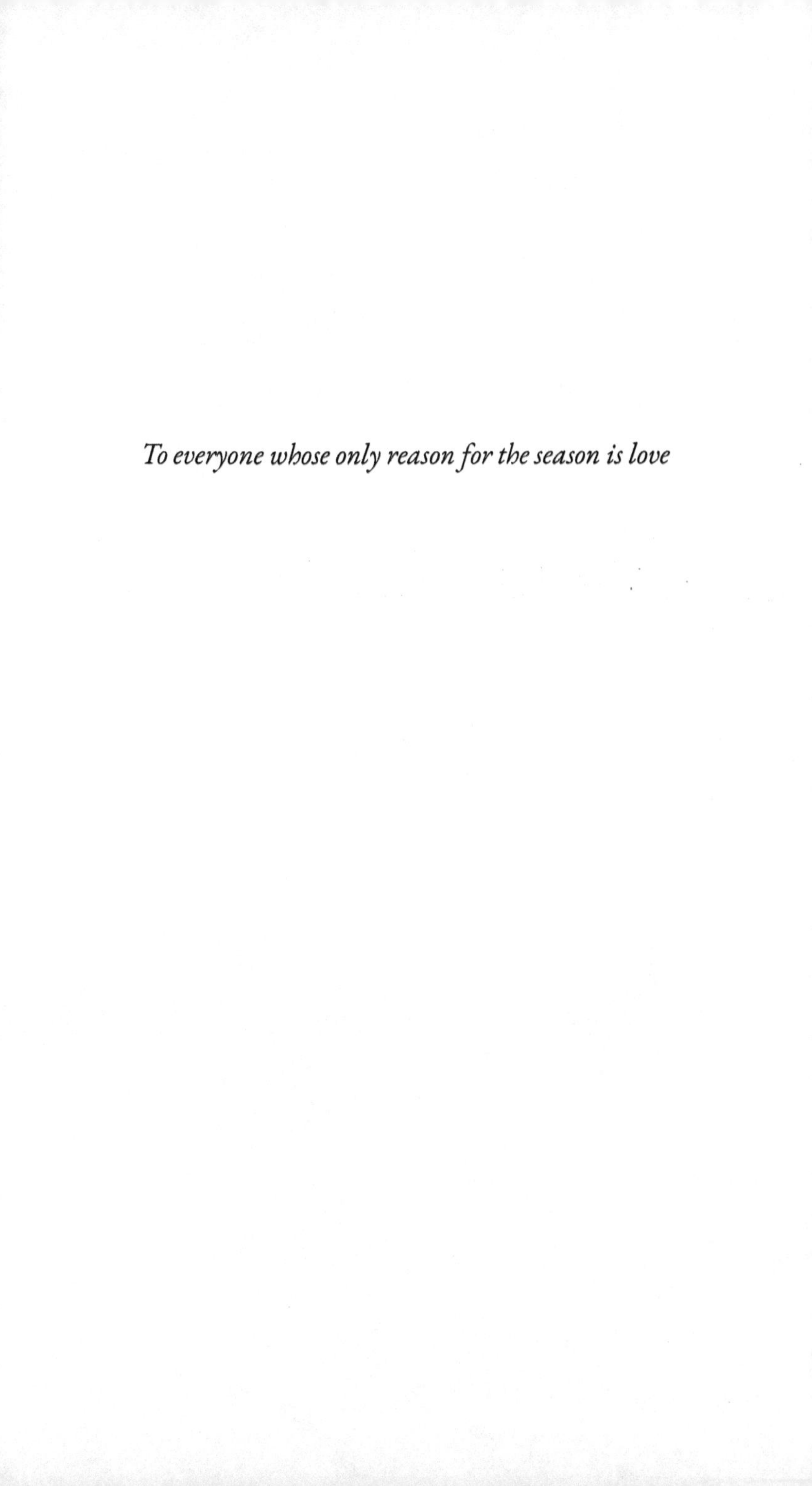

To everyone whose only reason for the season is love

content notes

This book includes discussions of agoraphobia and anxiety, death of a romantic partner (historical, off-page), swearing, and explicit sex. Reader discretion is advised.

Love Me Merrily is unapologetically an atheist holiday romance. Deconverting from Christianity as a teenager was one of the hardest—yet most liberating—transformations I've undergone in my life. It changed my entire worldview and rid me of the guilt and shame that was holding me back from living as my authentic self. While this book is not meant to besmirch those who find solace in religion, I hope it brings joy to my readers who are better people without it.

In a time where our constitutional rights are being systematically threatened, there are organizations fighting the good fight. If you would like to help preserve the separation between church and state in America, please consider supporting the Freedom From Religion Foundation (ffrf.org).

chapter
one

It's blasphemous to admit at this time of year, but the holidays are the worst. As I enter the grand ballroom of the Granite Grove Lodge—Yosemite's second-best hotel according to every travel magazine on my shit list—I find it hard to enjoy the festivities. Per company policy, the open hall has been decked out since November first: wreaths hanging in the windows, poinsettia centerpieces on every dining table, and a massive tree by the far wall, its needles barely visible underneath the obscene amount of ornaments, tinsel, and string lights.

My supervisor, the general manager, is out of town for the week, so as his direct report with the longest tenure, I'm filling in to run things while he's gone. That includes instructing all Granite Grove staff not to refer to our decor as explicitly Christmas-themed—even our tree is a "festive fir," gag. We wish our guests "happy holidays," but I've been working in Yosemite for over a decade, and I've yet to see any concerted efforts to celebrate other holidays. Sure, we host a Thanksgiving dinner and a quickly thrown together costume contest for Halloween, but the second the calendar month flips from ten to eleven, it's all about Christmas until the new year.

As I take in the lodge's color palette of red and green, I begrudgingly admit to myself that the decor does look phenomenal against the backdrop of the ballroom, with its stone interior and vaulted mahogany ceilings. The fire roaring in the granite hearth should be more than enough to keep me warm and cozy, yet my blood continues to run cold.

Because I hate every single winter holiday, and I hate Christmas most of all.

"Summer, where do these go?"

A young, bright-eyed woman gestures to the boxes off to the side, pulling out elaborate Venetian masks in wintry white and silver.

I sigh. As the front office manager, I usually remember the names of everyone working at Granite Grove. But now that I'm on a mission to be promoted to sales director by throwing our first-ever Merry Masquerade, I've had to hire additional seasonal staff, and I can't keep them straight. They're all right out of college, innocent and inexperienced, and I have little patience for their entry-level enthusiasm.

Twelve years ago, I was just like them. Before that dreaded day on the Matterhorn when the love of my life was struck by a large rock and died in my arms. Ryan and I were both experienced climbers—he was a pro at the top of his game, so it's not like we didn't know what we were doing. But I learned the devastatingly hard way that freak accidents don't just happen to amateurs.

"Tape those back up and lock them in the storage closet," I tell her, banishing the memory to the recesses of my mind. "There's not much space left, so the rest of the supplies will have to go in the break room."

My tone must have been steelier than I intended because the woman shuffles off with the box as fast as she can, avoiding eye contact. Jeez, I got to get it together. I may not feel any Christmas cheer, but if I keep snapping at Santa's little helpers, I can kiss my promotion goodbye because I'm going to find myself out of a job.

When I returned to work after Ryan's death, everyone treated me like I was bubble-wrapped. Who wouldn't have sympathy for the girl who held the back of her boyfriend's cracked skull as he bled out?

Most of those colleagues have moved away and moved on with their lives, while I remain frozen in time. Even on days when I'm feeling good and life seems completely normal, in a flash, I can be transported back to that mountain, and my whole mood is thrown off. But if I can't put on a happy face around people who don't know or care about my tragic backstory, then it will be my fault when I'm fired.

It's December twentieth. I only have to plaster on a smile for five more days, and then when the Merry Masquerade is over on Christmas Eve, I can take some much-needed paid time off and be a Scrooge in peace.

I'm going to be a beacon of hospitality. Right after I tell this red-headed trespasser to fuck off.

"Excuse me, sir?" I bark out to the only man not wearing the hotel's uniform. "The ballroom is closed until this evening." I check my watch, which reads a quarter after two. "Dinner starts in about three hours."

When I say he's red-headed, I don't mean he's a natural ginger. I mean his hair is dyed as brightly as the Santa hats we're forced to wear at the front desk this month. And his Kool-Aid hairdo isn't the only thing that stands out. He's also sporting ear gauges, a nose ring, and tattoos peeking out of his black hoodie.

We rarely get guys with this kind of street style—camping types are more minimalist—but there's something about his aesthetic that's familiar . . . do I know him?

I brush off the possibility, since it's obvious why his vibe is jogging my memory. Because Ryan used to look like this.

My evangelical family hated him, a rock-climbing rebel with an orange and yellow fauxhawk who shared my love for the "devil's music." Needless to say, I went very-low-contact when they couldn't even pretend to grieve his passing.

And here's this guy, someone who could be mistaken for Machine Gun Kelly, and all I can think is Ryan's ghost has come back to haunt me.

The hotel guest watches my expression shift from annoyance to apprehension and quickly explains himself. "I'm sorry, I didn't mean to intrude. You must be Summer McKenzie. We're scheduled to meet tomorrow morning, but I decided to drive up from Fresno early so I could check out the space."

"The space?" I repeat, racking my brain for why this dude waltzed into the ballroom. If he's interested in booking Granite Grove for a wedding, wouldn't his fiancée be with him?

"Yeah, for the Merry Masquerade. I'm John Beecher, the brand designer."

He sticks out his hand to shake mine, and it dawns on me where I've heard his name. The same name I've been emailing for months now, the one he shares with my primary point of contact. "Tania's brother? From Beecher Media."

John nods reassuringly, as if this isn't the first time this confusion has occurred. "Yes, Tania's the one who takes all the client calls. You *are* Summer, right?"

"The person who's in charge of this event but is apparently too scatterbrained to recall the co-owner of the marketing agency she hired. How did you guess?"

He averts his gaze. "Tania's always going on about how gorg—I mean, how great Summer looks on Zoom, so I figured you must be her."

John's face turns as red as his hair, and I must be blushing just as hard. Does he find me attractive?

Tania Beecher and I met under antagonistic circumstances two years ago—back when she stayed at Granite Grove during a corporate retreat and I thought she was a spoiled Bay Area coastal elite. Then my best friend—famed free solo climber Nolan Wells—fell in love with her, and eventually I changed my tune, once I saw her through his eyes. Now living ninety minutes south in Oakhurst, she still doesn't take naturally to the outdoors, but she's got a good heart and great taste in pop-punk music. And she finds every little quirk about Nolan endearing, even his disgusting habit of pissing in bottles when he's too lazy to leave the van on a climbing expedition. Now that they've been married for almost a year, I can't imagine any two people being a better fit together.

That's when it hits me. John Beecher isn't just Tania's younger brother. He's Nolan's brother-in-law.

Nolan only had one sibling—his twin, in fact—and that was Ryan. The man whose life I watched fade from his eyes. My first love who was gone way too soon.

chapter
two

"Are you alright?" John asks. "You look a little pale. Do you need me to get you something?"

He pulls out a dining chair and encourages me to take a seat. I appreciate his concern, though it embarrasses me more than anything. Even after years of therapy, I sometimes experience these out-of-body moments where the past comes rushing back and it feels like I can't breathe. But I'm not about to make that John's problem, even if he is now a part of Nolan's family.

"I got a bit lightheaded, that's all," I reassure John. "I've been running on fumes to plan this event perfectly. It must be catching up to me."

John returns my small smile as he scans the lobby, then he holds a hand up. "Wait here. I've got just the thing."

He jogs off to the hotel's vending machine, returning with two electric green bottles.

"Mountain Dew?" I say, incredulously. I have nothing against soda, but I usually go for a Mexican Coke when I can find one or a root beer if I'm in a sarsaparilla kind of mood. "I thought only hillbillies and hardcore video gamers drink this."

He chuckles, a bit sheepish. "If spending most of my free time gaming makes me hardcore, then I guess I uphold that stereotype." He twists the top off one bottle and hands it to me before throwing back a swig from his. "But it's my favorite soda that never fails to make me happy, and I figured you could use a pick-me-up."

"Thanks. You are right about that one." I tentatively take a sip, forgetting what Mountain Dew even tastes like, and discover it's surprisingly refreshing. Not the beverage I would ever gravitate toward, but John's kind gesture makes me like it more.

The rest of the staff has cleared out of the ballroom, and this massive space feels abnormally intimate when it's just the two of us. I'm sure there are a million items I could be checking off my to-do list, but for once, I'm not in a rush to complete them.

"You know," I muse, "if I went into business with my siblings, I would pull out all my hair, but you have such a calming presence. I get why Tania ditched her big corporate job to work with you."

John's eyes go wide. "Calming?"

"Yeah." I think back to what Tania's told me about her brother and business partner. "I joked once how she hasn't murdered you, and she emphatically declared I had it backward. That you were the grounded, down-to-earth one, and she was the basket case. I find that hard to believe about her, because she runs such a tight ship, but I agree with her assessment of you." I raise my plastic bottle. "If your pick-me-up method is any indicator."

He smiles, but it doesn't reach his eyes. "Tania's the

most competent person I know, but she exaggerates. If anyone is a basket case, it's me. I can barely leave my house."

His demeanor has turned visibly uncomfortable, so I decide it's best to return to business mode. "Well, driving all the way to Yosemite definitely counts as leaving the house. Where are your bags?" I ask. "Check-in is at four p.m., so we've got a couple of hours before you can get settled in your room, but you're welcome to chill in the lounge if you'd like."

"That's alright. I left my suitcases with the bell hop. I totally get it if you have more pressing priorities than the holiday party, but if you have some time, I'd love to ask you a few questions about the branding."

His request sounds innocuous, coming from a place of curiosity rather than one of urgency—which is a relief because the event is in five days, and I don't think my sanity could survive if I had to put out another figurative fire.

"Sure," I say hesitantly, "but should we wait for Tania to arrive? I wouldn't want her to be out of the loop. What's her ETA?"

John waves off my concern. "She and Nolan aren't coming until later—something about putting up the last of their Christmas decorations. For what it's worth, I'm not asking about logistics. The designs are locked and loaded, not to worry. There was a bit of context I felt was left out of the creative brief. Not about the what, but about the why. *Why* do you want to throw the Merry Masquerade?"

I blink. I'm not sure why this is an important tidbit for him to know, at least compared to the nitty-gritty details like the event's logo, color palette, and design assets. We're a popular hotel to book for holidays, and Christmas is this country's biggest holiday, so it's not some elaborate mystery.

"Oh, um," I stammer, coming up with a way to respond. "Winter in Yosemite is a wonder to behold, and our guests come to Granite Grove to celebrate in the most magical way possible."

John cocks his head. "Summer. I'm not your boss. I want your honest answer, not some bullshit boilerplate. Tania's in charge of PR spin, not me. You can keep it real."

Keep it real, eh? Everybody says that, especially when they ask me how I'm doing and don't accept "fine" as good enough. I grew to hate people checking on me after Ryan's accident. 'How are you *really* doing?' they'd insist. Oh, I don't know, Deborah from payroll—I cry myself to sleep at night, wishing that rock could have crushed my skull instead, and every day I don't jump off Half Dome out of survivor's guilt is a victory. I'm sorry, did I kill the mood during your lunch break? Then maybe next time, stick to eating your sad salad and leave me the hell alone.

Great. This man's just trying to do his job and understand the event's origin story, and I'm all fired up. But why? I've been itching to take on more responsibility and have pursued the sales director promotion for quite a while now, but why do I want the Merry Masquerade—out of all the potential events I could plan—to be my claim to fame?

Brewing resentment gurgles in my gut. The familiar feeling of being underestimated, whether it's by misogynistic climbers who assume I've never topped a 5.14 route or corporate drones who believe service work is easy work. But nothing gets me more riled up this time of year than constantly coming in second place.

"Okay, you asked for it. My one hundred percent honest answer is that I am sick and tired of Granite Grove getting overshadowed by the Sentinel House, and I want to take them down."

John spits out his Mountain Dew, mid-sip, scanning the ballroom to see if anyone else overheard my mic drop. "Wow . . . that was definitely not in the creative brief. Can I ask why?"

My hands ball into fists. "Sentinel always ranks as the number one hotel to stay in Yosemite Valley, and it feels rigged. They've had a long history of sucking up to investors, so they've been able to spend on top-dollar renovations and more luxurious amenities." I huff in pent-up frustration. "We offer a pretty bougie spa if I say so, but it doesn't have as many bells and whistles. Who needs cryotherapy anyway? If you want to shock your nervous system with frigid temperatures, you can walk outside."

Breathing deeply, I take a swig from my soda. "My point is, Sentinel has built a reputation of serving wealthy clientele, and it hosts a hoity-toity Christmas event that costs a whopping five hundred dollars to attend. Per person! It's ridiculous and completely antithetical to what this national park should be about. Yosemite is public land meant to be enjoyed by everybody, and the holidays should be no exception. I want to plan a kickass event that's accessible to the average American. So that's why you're here."

By the way his whole face lights up, I can tell John likes this answer better. It feels good to air this particular grievance. I have held a grudge against the Sentinel House my entire career, ever since I fell for Ryan during a whirlwind camping trip and started job-hunting in Yosemite so we could shack up together. Those early career conversations didn't go well: my Christian fundamentalist—aka fundie—family disapproved of me "living in sin," of course, but what I didn't expect was Ryan's wealthy parents snubbing their noses when a front desk clerk position at Granite Grove opened up. Ryan pushed me to apply, but the first words out of his mother's mouth were, "Isn't it a bit *common?*"

"What do you mean?" I had asked, bewildered at the time. "Granite Grove has a storied legacy, going back nearly a hundred years. It's a Yosemite institution!"

She had looked down her nose at me. "That's one way to describe it. Such a shame they haven't raised their prices high enough to keep out the riffraff. Why don't you work for the Sentinel House instead? Now, *that's* a hotel."

Thankfully, I didn't listen to a word she said. Ryan had warned me that he came from money, but he and Nolan couldn't care less about their future inheritance. All of us felt the same—we would much rather be climbing big walls than living the high life. And that hasn't changed.

John and I share a mischievous smile. Whether it's his punk-rock vibe or the neon beverage he's drinking, I get the sense that Ryan would like him. They both have the same stick-it-to-the-man energy that appeals to my rebellious streak.

"I'm on board," John says, enthusiasm reverberating in his voice. "Let's throw the merriest fucking masquerade this place has ever seen."

chapter
three

I fully intended to get John set up in the lounge and focus on finishing the rest of today's duties: confirming the vendors, testing the AV system, and setting up the photobooth area. But I kept procrastinating, preferring to hover around him.

Most adrenaline junkies and meditation-obsessed health nuts who visit Yosemite wouldn't find anything appealing about a grown man who plays video games and chugs green soda, but I find it so refreshing that John Beecher is nothing but himself. So when he asked me for the grand tour of Granite Grove, my mouth blurted out "of course" before my brain could shut it down.

I begin by introducing him to the facilities—the industrial kitchen that keeps hundreds of guests fed each day, and the business center that will be taking care of John's printing needs for the event. And when he asks to see the grounds, I escort him around the property, making sure to grab two Granite Grove waterproof jackets for us before stepping outside.

"Thanks," he says sheepishly as he throws the jacket

over his hoodie. "You would think after visiting here once before, I would be better prepared, but I don't get out much."

We crunch through the snow covering the expansive lawn behind the hotel, and John's comment distracts me from stressing about the darkening, gloomy skies. The weather can turn for the worse in no time, and the last thing I need before this holiday party is a blizzard barring guests from entering the valley.

"You've been to Granite Grove before?" I exclaim.

"For Tania's wedding, on Valentine's Day," he says, pointing to the clearing ahead. "We had the ceremony right over there."

Duh. John was also at the wedding. Nolan invited so many of his climbing buddies that I must not have noticed him among the sea of other dudes. "I'm surprised I didn't meet you then. Were you one of the groomsmen?"

He shakes his head, pulling his jacket tighter to ward off the windchill. "Nolan was nice to offer, but I . . . I used to get really anxious in social settings. I was totally fine attending as a guest and blending into the crowd."

I bark out a laugh before I can stop myself. "Sorry. I just find it hard to picture you blending into anything when you're tatted neck-to-fingertip and your hair is as attention-grabbing as a fire truck."

"You got me there," he concedes, gliding his hand through his candy-apple locks. "To be fair, I was less noticeable when it was dyed black back then." He pauses, like he's unsure if he should continue. "I do remember you though."

I fidget with my jacket zipper. "Are you sure you're not mixing me up with the more eye-catching blondes who were there?" There's no way I could have stood out, not when Tania's bridesmaids included Alex Waterston-Gardner, the mega-famous supermodel, and Casey Holbright, her equally stunning stylist. Tania may have been the center of attention as the bride, but her celebrity friends were a very close second.

"No, it was definitely you," John insists. "Because during happy hour, I asked my sister who was in the ice-blue dress and when she said Summer, I thought that made perfect sense. It was a cold day, in the middle of winter, and it was like you brought the sun out."

The compliment stops me in my tracks, and not just because I've always found it bizarre that my parents named their December baby Summer. I admit I wasn't in the best headspace during Tania and Nolan's wedding. I was so happy that my best friend had found his life partner, but I was also devastated that I would go the rest of my life without his brother as *my* partner. If Ryan was still alive, I would have been making googly eyes with him as he stood beside Nolan as his best man, but instead I cried as inconspicuously as I could and left the reception early.

But John doesn't need to know how much of a mess I was that day, not when he makes it sound like he laid eyes on a goddess.

"It's a shame we didn't meet then," I say, trying to sound lighthearted. "That would have been one hell of a pick-up line."

John trips over himself, stumbling into the snow. A sound escapes me, half-laugh, half-concern that he took a tumble. I extend my hand to help him to his feet, and for a brief moment, I'm grateful we're not wearing gloves. His fingers are like icicles after bracing his fall and without thinking, I hold onto them to warm them up. We stand like that, his hand in mine, cheeks flushed, until he pulls back in embarrassment.

It's his self-consciousness I find so endearing. I've met plenty of climbers and elite athletes who can't see past their own egos, but most spend so much time alone or in male-dominated spaces that they lack major game. They can climb thousand-foot walls without a care in the world, but talking to a woman is what sends them into a tailspin. They don't realize what they consider to be a fault is what we find most attractive.

It's not the only thing I find attractive about John either. As we walk back to the lodge, my gaze settles on his sharp jaw and slightly crooked nose—even the red hair falling into his eyes makes me wonder what it would feel like to run my fingers through it.

In the decade since I lost Ryan, I've tried going on casual dates, but I never connected with anyone I could see myself committing to. Not to mention, working in hospitality means that most people I interact with are seasonal employees or hotel guests visiting on vacation. No point in getting attached if they're staying temporarily.

But John Beecher is unique in ways that are hard to explain. I've met many good-looking guys, but there's something under the surface that intrigues me. We've known of each other without really knowing each other, and I find myself wanting more.

It's about half-till four, so I offer to check John in early so he can beat the afternoon rush. But as we enter the lobby, his phone rings, blaring an old song by Bring Me the Horizon. The kind of blasphemous music I loved listening to just to piss off my parents.

"Sorry, it's Tania. Let me take this." He raises the phone

to his heavily pierced ear. "Hey, sis, are you on your way?" His face falls. "What do you mean? Is he okay?"

My stomach drops. I'm assuming the 'he' in this conversation is Nolan Wells. And while John knows him as Tania's husband, Nolan has been my best friend for over a decade. I avoid my own family like the plague, so Nolan is like the sibling I never had. The only person on earth who understands what losing Ryan feels like, who grieves him as deeply as I do.

And if one more Wells brother disappears from my life, I don't know what I'll do.

Between my pounding heart and the blood rushing to my ears, I can't make out the rest of the conversation. Images from the past flood my brain: an ambulance transporting a body beyond saving, a sink stained red from the blood I scrubbed off my hands, the pastor at the funeral spouting off platitudes that filled me with rage—

What the hell am I waiting for? I have to get out of here.

"Summer, wait! Where are you going?" John grabs my arm, and I whip around, taken aback by how fast tears start streaming down my face.

"Nolan," I gasp. "I have to go. There's no time—"

His confusion evolves into understanding at the sight of my freakout. He pulls me in, wrapping his arms around me. "He's fine. Nolan is safe. Tania was just telling me he slipped while stringing Christmas lights around their house, and he sprained his ankle. She's running late because she's taking him to urgent care, but it's a minor injury. He's okay." He smooths my hair until I stop shaking. "If anything, Tania's more annoyed at him because if he used a ladder instead of climbing the damn walls, this wouldn't have happened."

I hiccup a small laugh, sinking into John's embrace. Of

course, Nolan would free solo his own house. I always knew the Wells brothers would be the death of me, but I didn't think I'd lose my mind over some silly holiday decorations.

I'm surprised how quickly John jumped in to calm me down and how natural it feels to be held by him. Hanging around Ryan's friends after his death was too painful: I turned down their hugs left and right until I got used to not being consoled—and now I fear John has set the bar too high. He breathes deeply with me as my heart rate returns to normal and doesn't pull away until I'm ready.

"Thank you," I say, taking a step back before I'm consumed by his irresistible cologne—something earthy with a hint of spice. "I, um, tend to jump to the worst possible conclusion."

John scratches the back of his head. "Nolan's talked about his brother. And how close he is with you. It makes total sense that you'd worry about him."

Ah. Of course he knows about Ryan and our history. We had only been dating a few months, so my name was never included in the news articles about his death, but it's not like it's a secret. Especially not with the people I consider family.

With anyone else, I would feel violated by someone knowing about my deepest wounds before I have the chance to divulge them on my own terms. I don't air out my dirty laundry to everyone I meet. But there's something comforting about not needing to explain myself for once. John and I are part of the same inner circle, and though he doesn't know the gruesome details, he seems like the kind of person who takes care of others, no questions asked.

Embarrassed by my ability to panic at the slightest provocation, I let out a sigh. Time to stop making mountains out of molehills. "How about we get you checked in?" I walk John over to the front desk. "Will Tania need to cancel her reservation now that Nolan's out of commission? It looks like she booked the honeymoon suite, but I can transfer the room to you if they can no longer make it. I'd hate to see that claw-footed tub go to waste."

"No, that's okay. Tania said she'd be late, so I'm hoping she can drive up later tonight or early tomorrow at the latest." He glances back at the darkening sky. "As long as the weather holds up."

We share a grimace, both hoping for the best. When I checked the forecast this morning, it wasn't promising, but Yosemite winters are known for unpredictable conditions. Fingers crossed a blizzard doesn't topple my well-laid plans like a house of cards.

I fetch John's bags from the bell hop, shocked to see her wheel out a cart stacked with suitcases. "Were you planning on moving in?" I tease, pushing the cart toward his room despite his insistence that he can manage the task himself.

John goes red, and I start to see the benefits of taking a liking to a pale guy like him. I'm used to being around leathery dudes who think sunscreen will worsen their climbing skills. With no tan to hide his blushing cheeks, John comes across as even more adorable.

"I guess I take after Tania. She taught me to be prepared for anything." He presses the button to call the elevator. "And I figured I could get some painting done in my downtime."

"That's so cool!" I beam as he helps me get the cart into the lift. "Well, you can't beat Yosemite for creative inspiration. I'm not artistic, but if all goes well with the masquerade and I get promoted to sales director, I want to hire someone to host paint-and-sip parties. Many of our guests want to enjoy the outdoors without having to be *in* the outdoors, you know?"

John chuckles. "That's definitely me. Living to your fullest potential does not have to involve hiking. Gimme a gorgeous view and good enough latency to play my first-person shooter games, and I'm a happy camper."

We make our way to his room, and John swipes his key before holding the door open so I can get his stuff inside. It's no honeymoon suite, but the standard room holds the same woodsy charm. A warm and rustic color palette, a plush bed, and a small balcony overlooking the valley. Way more extravagant than staff housing.

"What you said earlier," John says softly as we admire the mountaintops in the distance. "About not being artistic. I don't think that's true. Art is not limited to painting or pottery. Creating events and experiences people love is art too. You'd make an awesome sales director, so give yourself more credit. You're doing great, Summer."

His words are so simple, and yet they hit my chest, making me want to double over from the impact. It's not like I don't get praised for the work I do, but I have a hard time internalizing positive feedback. My family didn't think I was great for leaving their religion, Ryan's parents didn't think I was great for taking a service job, and I didn't think I was great when I couldn't save my boyfriend from getting his head bashed in by a loose rock. I haven't felt worthy of anything for a long time.

But in this moment, John Beecher makes me feel like something better may be on the horizon. Even if the snow is coming down hard, and the actual horizon looks like a bad omen.

As long as me and John are on the same team, I have hope we can make this masquerade merry after all.

chapter
four

My hopes are dashed the next day when I wake up and see the weather has taken a turn for the absolute worst. Visibility has plummeted as walls of snow pelt Granite Grove, and when I check the road service alerts, they verify what I already know to be true: nobody will be getting in or out of the valley today.

The silver lining to this terrible timing is that today is my birthday. Employee housing leaves a lot to be desired, so every year for my birthday, I spend some of my modest savings on a room at the lodge. I usually can't take paid time off until after Christmas, but after constantly being disregarded while everyone's focused on their holiday obligations, I stopped waiting to treat myself. And a hard day's work is more bearable when you know a California king size bed is calling your name.

It's a shame I won't be snuggling under the covers of said bed this morning, not when I'm pulling double duty: simultaneously planning the Merry Masquerade, which is happening in T-minus four days, and making sure the guests don't go completely stir-crazy.

My branding meeting with Beecher Media is at nine a.m. sharp, so I head down early to make myself a quick breakfast in the break room beforehand. I scarf down a bagel with cream cheese, wondering whether Tania made it in last night.

But on the way to our designated conference room, I catch sight of John in the business center—sans his sister—talking to the clerk Rebekah with a frown on his face.

"Needed to print some last-minute handouts before our session?" I say jovially. When John's frown deepens, I realize whatever's going on is not a laughing matter.

"Tania's snowed in, so I came to pick up the menus and seating chart," John explains, "but the order was never printed. Even though I placed it weeks ago."

Alarm bells start going off in my head, but I'm determined not to overreact so early in the day when there are a million other things to be concerned about—like what the hell I'm going to do if the vendors can't enter the valley. "It must have gotten lost in the shuffle. The software we use is in need of a major upgrade, which I was going to prioritize in the new year once the holiday mayhem is over. But we still have the files, right? We can put a rush on the print job now."

Rebekah taps her nails on the counter, the metallic purple polish contrasting beautifully against her dark brown skin. "About that . . . we were supposed to receive a shipment of new toner today, but that delivery is delayed because of the storm. The ink was already running low, and now . . . it's definitely out."

I groan, running my hand over my face. I knew the snowstorm would bring chaos into my life, but I didn't think I'd have to worry about fucking printer ink.

"What can we do?" John asks, echoing the desperation I

feel. "Are there office supplies at a general store somewhere?"

I shake my head. "Even if we had better visibility, the Valley Store only carries the essentials. It might have toner for the average person's rinky-dink printer at home, but it won't be compatible with our commercial printers. And the seating chart is supposed to be printed on a giant foam board atop an easel." I sigh, considering the ramifications. "If people don't know where they're sitting, and it's a free-for-all, there's bound to be confusion and conflict. Guests will start stealing chairs from other tables to fit their friends, and the staff won't know where those with serious food allergies are seated. It will be a gigantic mess."

John nods, resigned. "Yeah, I never understood the point of seating charts until Tania and Nolan's wedding ballooned to two hundred people with all the climbing friends he invited. Designing the chart was a cakewalk compared to the stress Tania had to go through to organize it." He raps his knuckles on the counter, the lightbulb going off in his brain. "Duh! I can't believe I forgot—I'm now experienced in this department. I can help. Designing these assets by hand is going to be a pain, but between the business center's resources and all the art supplies I over-packed for this trip, we should have what we need."

"By hand?" I repeat, eyes wide. "The Merry Masquerade is expecting four hundred people—that's double the size of your sister's wedding. How the hell are you going to create that many menus in just four days?"

He doesn't miss a beat. "I've taken quite a few typog-raphy and calligraphy classes as part of my corporate-mandated professional development, so I'm not bragging when I say my handwriting skills are damn good. Once I take care of the text, I can teach some basic designs to as many team members as you can spare. Simple holiday stuff, like snowflakes, Santa hats, and Christmas trees. We can form an assembly line, so everybody can get comfortable with their one design. While they're cranking out the menus, I can create the seating chart. Will that work?"

I can tell John's background designing for scrappy tech startups has come in handy. He's used to brainstorming big ideas on tiny budgets. From the way he's ready to roll up his sleeves—and show off those toned forearms—he's the kind of man who delivers solutions.

Okay, enough drooling over John's forearms—even though they have me wondering what physical activity he partakes in to sculpt them like that. Gaming's a handheld hobby, but *Halo* doesn't give you muscles.

"It better work," I reply, "because no other options are coming to me. I'm going to be pulled in a million directions today, so I trust you. Let's make it happen."

John and I quickly touch base on the rest of the items on the branding meeting's agenda, but this new project clearly takes higher priority, so I get him set up in the ballroom with a small team of junior staff.

Tania mentioned when she and John used to work together at that hot tech company Habituall, he was a freelance designer, so it was her responsibility to manage the in-house brand team. But watching him lead Granite Grove's employees is like that time I witnessed a mountain lion taking down a deer. He's a natural. Emotionally, I aged decades after Ryan's death, so my fuse with entry-level twenty-somethings is a lot shorter these days, but John has the patience of a saint. He answers their inane questions—yes, those markers are permanent—and gives them words of encouragement as they perfect their techniques.

"It's okay if the snowflakes aren't perfect," he tells the

staff. "Each one is supposed to be unique." He turns to me and mutters under his breath. "And if they come out a little squiggly, we'll call them rustic."

I laugh. "That was Tania's favorite word during wedding planning. Every little error or mishap contributed to the rustic charm." With John's artistic assembly line firing on all cylinders, I'm reassured that regardless of what happens with this event, at least he has this element under control.

"Alright," I say, clapping my hands. "Looks like you've got this handled, so I'll leave you to it. Thanks so much. You're a lifesaver." I reach out to grip his upper arm, appreciating the firm definition underneath his navy sweater.

He holds onto the spot I touched, as if I'm the one doing him a favor. "No worries. I'm happy to help."

I give a grateful smile before turning on my heel. But as I'm about to exit the ballroom, one of the staff calls out, "Oh, and happy birthday, Summer!"

"Birthday?" John echoes, shocked. "Were you not going to say anything this whole time? We should throw you a party tonight!"

"It's not a big deal," I reassure everybody. "I'm used to people being busy with holiday stuff. Honestly, I tend to forget about it." Not honest, if we're counting the fact that I never forget to treat myself to a room at the hotel I help oversee, but that would make me sound more pathetic.

"Birthdays aren't burdens or impositions," John insists. "You deserve to be celebrated." His tone isn't sad or pitying, but it's his word choice that catches me off guard. He didn't say I deserve to celebrate. He said I deserve to *be celebrated*. The former implies that I'm the one taking action, making things happen. But being celebrated sounds like letting others take care of me for once, and I like the sound of it. Too bad there's way too much to get done today.

"Let's grab drinks, after this"—I wave my hand at the flurry of menu designing—"is all wrapped up."

He flashes a toothy grin. "Sounds like a plan."

THE DAY FLIES by as expected. As stressed as I am by the horrid weather, checking hourly for updates on when this storm is going to blow over, the one thing I don't have to worry about is the branding. There would be no way I would have finished four hundred menus and a massive seating chart in four days, let alone one, but John and his assembly line of assistants completed the task faster than I thought was physically possible.

In fact, when I return to the ballroom after the sun has set, I find John at a window working on an entirely different art piece.

"What in the world is this?" I say in awe. On an easel he has a watercolor painting of Yosemite Falls. I've seen my fair share of landscapes while working in the valley, but I'm blown away by John's ability to capture color. How do you even paint something that's white? He's created a winter wonderland, with a large pile of snow at the base of the upper falls. It practically sparkles where the waterfall mist freezes into what's known as frazil ice, clinging to the rock like decorative lace.

John paints the finishing touches on the sixteen-by-twenty canvas, placing his monogram signature in the bottom-right corner. "I can't stand driving, but as I was making my way through the valley, I got such a kick out of this view. It's like the waterfall's making a snow cone."

I grin from ear to ear. "That's what we call it. The snow cone can reach hundreds of feet high. It's one of my favorite parts of the season."

John matches my smile, filled with pride at a job well done. "Then it's a good thing it's yours. I'll hold onto it until it dries to keep it safe, but it'll be ready tomorrow. Happy birthday, Summer."

It takes a few beats for his words to register, and then I seize up. "Oh, no. I can't. John, this is too much."

He blurts out a *pssshhh* sound. "Of course you can. Otherwise, I wasted two hours and risked carpal tunnel syndrome for your ungrateful ass."

"Point taken," I say, laughing. "Thank you. I haven't received a birthday gift that hasn't doubled as a Christmas gift in a long time."

Partially true, since I haven't received *any* gifts in a long time. Before Ryan passed, he and Nolan were sweethearts who loved being generous with the people around them. We had started dating in the spring—not even close to my birthday—but the Wells brothers never needed a reason to bake me dessert in their van's makeshift kitchen. But afterwards, Nolan threw himself into his obsession with climbing El Capitan, and I told him we were getting too old for presents anyway. The truth was, it was too painful for me to reciprocate, because Nolan's birthday was my eternal reminder that Ryan wasn't around to celebrate his.

By now, the rest of the staff has wrapped up their shifts, so it's just the two of us in this expansive space. Before I can talk myself out of it, I pull John in for a hug, squeezing tight. "Helping me out today was gift enough, but this is beyond. I love it so much."

He murmurs into my ear, sending a shiver down my

spine. "I have a feeling you've been going beyond for everyone else for a while. It's the least I can do."

With no one around, we're not in a rush to end our embrace. As John strokes my hair, I notice similar blonde strands from a much smaller portrait peeking out from under his pile of paper.

"What's that?" I step back and reach for the obscured painting.

"It's nothing, let me . . . " John stammers, trying to beat me to it, but I grab the sheet before he can, holding it out of reach so I can get a better look. It's not just the hair that's the same as mine—I also recognize the freckles on my cheeks, the way my nose crinkles when somebody makes me laugh, the jacket I was wearing yesterday. It's unmistakable.

"That's me."

John interprets my shock as concern, rubbing his eyes with embarrassment. "If I deny it, I'm a liar, but if I admit it, I'm a creep. Please, let's pretend this never happened."

I instinctively hold the painting closer to my chest. "But I don't want to. John, this is *gorgeous*. The way the sun circles my head like a halo . . . I don't think I've ever looked this good in my life."

John exhales a scoff. "That's not possible. Nothing I paint could ever do the real you justice. You put Yosemite's beauty to shame."

Half of me is reeling. I literally met this man yesterday. He managed to squeeze in a portrait of me while also painting me a birthday gift and keeping our branding from going off the rails. Even if he was hopped up on caffeine all day to keep his energy high, how can I have possibly made that much of an impact on him?

And yet, the other half of me completely understands this connection because it feels like the most natural thing in the world. He's my friend's brother. My best friend's brother-in-law. One of the few people who already knew about my deepest grief before our paths crossed. I know it would sound ridiculous if I said it out loud, but John Beecher feels like family to me.

Which is why I don't hesitate to kiss him.

He freezes when I approach, as if expecting me to slap him for imitating my likeness without my expressed consent. But once my lips land on his, he melts underneath my touch. His relief is palpable, and he clings to me like he's afraid of being swept away by the snowstorm.

Now that our brains have absorbed the initial shock that our attraction is indeed mutual, our bodies have a chance to catch up. I've had a few lackluster kisses over the past decade, so I expect a little awkwardness, but John's ability to anticipate my needs before I do is uncanny. His thumb pulls at my bottom lip, requesting entry, and the moment my mouth opens for him, his tongue meets mine, igniting me from the inside out. He groans, cradling my face firmly in his hands, and I find myself snaking mine under his sweater. His abs tense, and as he pulls me closer, I can tell that's not the only body part that's hard.

Just as I'm about to suggest we take things up to my hotel room, we're interrupted by one of the most grating sounds known to man: the happy birthday song.

We break apart as the front desk staff pours through the ballroom, carefully guarding the cake they're carrying, which looks like it's been set ablaze. Did they need to light a candle for each of the thirty-three years I've been alive? I fear the smoke detectors are going to go off.

"Happy birthday, dear Summerrrrr," they sing. "Happy birthday to youuuuuuu."

"What is this all for?" I say. "We're not a cake-and-ice-cream kind of workplace."

The gaggle of young employees starts cutting the cake and handing out slices. "It was John's idea," says their leader wielding the knife. "He said it's not fair that people with December birthdays get passed over during the holiday party planning. So this is thanks for everything you do, Summer."

"Thank you." I'm stunned. I turn to John, who's holding my Yosemite landscape in front of his body to hide the fact that he's got a raging hard-on. "That was really thoughtful."

John coughs, adjusting his pants behind the painting. "I, um, honestly forgot until just now."

I bet. As we dig into the cake—red velvet with cream cheese frosting, my favorite—I accept that the birthday surprise is probably for the best. Things were getting hot and heavy, and from the way we were *this-close* to ripping each other's clothes off, John and I were moving way too fast. I'm already getting attached to having him around, which is only going to end in heartache. After the Merry Masquerade is over, John will head back to Fresno, and I'll be on my own—again.

As I shove decadent deliciousness into my mouth, the sad realization sets in: like my cake, I can't have John Beecher and keep him too.

chapter
five

When I peer outside the window the next morning, it's more of the same. We're not in the thick of an active blizzard, but I know for a fact that the roads will remain closed today. *Fuck*.

I can only hope my weather app is correct and the forecast is supposed to improve this afternoon. The Merry Masquerade is in three days, and busting my ass for this event will be meaningless if it has to be canceled.

Eager to have a reason to spend extra time on my appearance, I'm applying a natural face to accompany my casually windswept waves when my phone buzzes.

JOHN BEECHER

Tania is snowed in like the rest of us, so this might be the first event I'm planning without her.

His text surprises me. On the surface, John's simply relaying that half of Beecher Media is still missing in action, but I can feel his trepidation. He's been tied professionally at the hip to his older sister, and it must be unnerving to be unable to follow her lead. Sure, she can advise him from a distance, but John's the boots on the ground. When it comes to make-or-break decisions in the moment, he's the one who will be making them.

SUMMER MCKENZIE

Well, if this weather doesn't let up, there won't be a masquerade, merry or not.

JOHN BEECHER

That's okay. We're just camping.

SUMMER MCKENZIE

Camping? I'd like to think the lodge is more luxurious than tent-living.

JOHN BEECHER

I meant the kind of camping that happens in games like Call of Duty. We sit tight until an opportunity shows itself when we can make a move. So how can I help today?

I smile. I never thought an outdoor enthusiast and an indoor cat could speak the same language, but here we are. Even when Mother Nature has a personal vendetta against me, John's first instinct is to make my life easier.

The guests are getting restless, so I instruct him to bring his art supplies to the hotel lobby. When we meet downstairs, I walk him through the game plan.

"To keep everyone from rioting due to boredom, you'll be in charge of hosting Granite Grove's very first paint-and-sip while I'm occupied with assembling the party favors. Your landscape skills are too good not to capitalize on them," I say, avoiding his gaze. Our kiss yesterday was so good I forgot my own birthday, so it's clear that painting isn't the only thing John Beecher is a prodigy at.

"Summer, look at me," John says, leaning down and craning his body to infiltrate my field of vision. "Was it that bad or that good?"

'It' being the kiss that rocked my world. There's hope in his voice, but also uncertainty. He really wants to know. All of a sudden, my urge to reassure him supplants my awkwardness. I can't have him thinking I didn't enjoy his lips on mine with every fiber of my being.

"That good," I insist. "And I know it doesn't count for much because I don't have a lot of experience, but it was the best I've had in a long, long time."

John beams brighter than the sun peeking out of the clouds. "Same. I could say I lack experience because I'm as selective about my dates as I am about my clients, but that would be a lie. It's . . . it's hard for me to leave my house."

I bite my lip, concerned that I'm asking way too much of him today. Working with my team to design menus is one thing, but teaching beginner painting techniques to our cooped-up patrons isn't exactly a walk in the national park. "Are you going to be alright? I don't want you to think I'm abandoning you to the wolves."

"Lucky for me there are no wolves in Yosemite—and yes, I looked it up." John scratches the base of his head, a nervous habit of his I've noticed. "I've done a lot of work in therapy over the past year. Once I'm at my destination, I can usually manage my social anxiety without any issues. It's the getting there that's the hardest part. I'm not expecting anything else to happen between us, but if I knew you kissed like that, I might have conquered my fear of stepping outside the front door by now."

I had no intention of going any further with him, until he showed that level of vulnerability—first thing in the morning, no less. Maybe it wouldn't kill us to get our hopes up.

"If I were you, I'd keep the possibility open on something happening." I swivel to take in the staff hovering around us, awaiting today's instructions. "Not now, but come find me in the afternoon and force me to take a break, will you?"

He gives me a little salute. "You got it." He practically skips off, and I can't help but feel the same lightness. Staring at my jam-packed agenda on my phone, I start to think I can conquer anything in my path too.

WITH THE ANTICIPATION of spending more quality time with John, you would think I'd have been on pins and needles all day. But that's the thing with work—when it consumes you during periods of crunch time, it's hard for your brain to hold onto anything else.

Which is why I jump out of my skin when John taps me on the shoulder while I'm wrapping festive ribbons around Granite Grove's Yosemi-tree plant cube party favors.

"Whoa there!" he exclaims, taking several steps back so he's not impaled by my scissors. "If you ever see a ghost, you'd kill him twice."

I clutch my chest with relief. "Why do I feel like you'd make a good ghost?"

He grins, unoffended. "I'm already a pale, lanky creature who slips by people unnoticed. Tania used to call me Slenderman because I was obsessed with horror video games."

I snicker at the comparison. Who knew that a woman like me—raised by fire-and-brimstone fundies—would be crushing hard on an alt-rock designer who compares himself to a demon? My family would have the exorcism planned before the sun went down.

My morbid curiosity gets the best of me. Tania has mentioned in passing that her parents are Christian conservatives, but I was under the impression the Beecher kids broke that mold. "You don't believe in ghosts, do you?"

John's face scrunches in confusion. "Like for real? Absolutely not. I'm an atheist. The only thing waiting for me when I die are the worms in the dirt I get tossed into." He pauses, as if belatedly realizing who he's talking to. "Sorry. I'm flippant about my own death, but I don't mean to be crass about it."

I shake my head. "No. Don't do that. When Ryan died, I got so sick of people handling me with kid gloves, even though I got up close and personal with his brain matter. Nothing deconverted me faster than people telling me it was all part of god's plan. What horseshit. That's the real blasphemy, thinking some omnipotent being cracked open a twenty-three-year-old's skull to teach us some grand lesson. I broke off ties with my evangelical family and never stepped foot in a church again after his funeral. My faith died with him, and unlike Ryan, I never missed it."

Heat rising to my cheeks, I brace myself for John's pity. But what I notice more than his polite sympathy is his pride. While his reasons for abandoning his religion are different, we made the same transformation, and we're better for it.

John glances around the room to make sure no one's around to eavesdrop. "So what the fuck are you doing planning Yosemite's most ambitious Christmas party? I mean, I get wanting to be promoted, but there's got to be other ways of going about it."

I let out an exasperated huff. "Why should Christians get to have all the fun? Yes, the chokehold the holiday has on this time of year is annoying, sucking the air out of absolutely everything else, but the Merry Masquerade is my way of reclaiming Christmas on my own terms."

We head out of the office and into the lobby. If my eyes aren't deceiving me, John is making a great effort trying not to hold my hand while I'm on the job. Which reminds me . . .

"So, what's the plan?" I check my watch. "I can probably afford an hour-long break."

"Make it three." When my eyes bug out of my head, he laughs. "I'm serious. You've been working so hard on this event that you deserve to take the rest of the afternoon off. Not to mention, your manager isn't even here—it's not like anyone is going to stop you."

He has a point. I gaze around the lodge, a weight lifting off my shoulders. I can take a breather, and the world won't crumble around me for once? Imagine that.

"What other holiday traditions do you want to reclaim?" John asks, genuinely interested. "My parents are spiritual but not overly religious, so I never felt that I couldn't do Christmas my way. But if you weren't allowed to have any other reason for the season, let's fix that. Right now."

I rack my brain, whirring with possibilities. If I could celebrate Christmas without all the lord-and-savior stuff, what would that look like?

"I want a hot toddy," I say, the first thing bursting out of my mouth. "Because I was told alcohol was the devil's drink. And I would like to play modern Christmas songs— not the stale gospel that puts me to sleep. Oh, and snow angels! Those were allowed, but I just can't stand the connotation. Why does waving your limbs around have to be a religious thing?"

After blurting out my laundry list, I expect John to look at me like I've lost my mind. But instead, he's bouncing on the balls of his feet. He's as excited as I am to let loose.

"Let's do it," he says, pumping his fist. "I've got a Blue-tooth speaker in my bag, and as long as we don't stray too far from the lodge, it should work. One atheist-friendly Christmas montage, coming right up."

The bartender on shift in the lounge makes us two hot toddies to go, and we bundle up in the proper outerwear, carrying our thermoses outside. The fire pits aren't turned on, but thankfully, the weather app was on-point, and the snow has slowed to a light dusting.

"The worst should be over now," I say, gesturing to the clouds, which have lightened to a less ominous gray. "I'm looking forward to getting the bonfires going again for the guests."

John sets up his speaker on the stone pit. "Given how packed that bar was, I'm glad they've found another way to entertain themselves. More Christmas magic for the two of us." He puts on the most sacrilegious playlist he can find, and the sounds of heavy guitar and angsty vocals echo through our slice of the valley.

"It's the *Punk Goes Christmas* album," he explains. "Not a 'O Come, All Ye Faithful' in sight."

The songs are covers of Christmas classics by the type of bands I fell in love with behind my family's back. The music's like a healing balm, and before I know it, I'm head-banging like I'm up against the barricade of the Warped Tour concerts I was forbidden to attend as a teen.

"You know, Tania and I didn't get off on the right foot when we first met. But when we discovered we were both fans of AFI, that's when we figured out we had more in common than we thought."

John smiles behind his hot toddy as he takes a sip. "She told me. All I kept thinking was you had great taste." His expression shifts to something more serious, more earnest. "I can see why you were so protective of Nolan in the early days of them dating. Why you're still so protective of him now. After losing Ryan, it makes sense that you'd never want to lose Nolan too."

Hearing John say Ryan's name is more soothing than the snare drums coming through the speaker. One of the things that drove me up a wall after his death was how quickly people started referring to him euphemistically. It was always "him" or "Nolan's brother," no matter how much I would scream that Ryan Wells was—and is—his name.

"They're the closest I have to family. Ryan's passing doesn't become easier the less he's brought up, so thank you for not shying away from mentioning him. We can't honor the dead if we can't even talk about them."

We stomp around in a circle, enjoying the way the snow crunches underneath our boots. "That's why atheism is the only worldview that's made sense to me," John says. "Religion can be hope for many people, but after having a brush with death myself, I find it liberating that this is the one life we get. It's a reminder to make the most of it, especially when my agoraphobia is holding me back. When there's no heaven, I have extra incentive to get the fuck out of my house and experience everything this world has to offer."

I reach for his hand, taking a moment to warm his icy fingers between mine. It's the first time he's specifically referred to his fear of leaving the safety of his home as agoraphobia—and that he's alluded to the incident that may have spurred it. He said he had a brush with death? I'm torn between wanting to ask him about it and giving him the space to address it on his own.

But before I can decide, John's on to the next item on our agenda. "Alright, about those snow angels."

I gulp down what's left of my hot toddy and set our empty thermoses next to the speaker. "We gotta call them something else, though. There have to be other triangle-shaped things we can imitate."

John ponders for a few beats. "What about wizards? Nothing more magical than sorcery."

I kick up some powder in my excitement. "Yes! The perfect fuck you to my family who refused to read or watch *The Lord of the Rings* because they thought Tolkien wasn't a devout enough Christian."

"Woof. The same author who invented a savior who was resurrected? I'm sorry, that sounds like a terrible environment to grow up in. Snow Gandalfs, it is."

"Snow Gandalfs!" I shout, as we fall back into the surprisingly plush snow. Side by side, we wave our arms and legs to make our wizardly figures. I should be freezing, but between the whiskey warming my belly and the small act of belated rebellion fueling me, I feel invigorated.

On our next upswing, John suddenly grabs my hand and meets my gaze with the same intensity we exchanged before our first kiss. In a few moves, we bridge the gap, crashing into each other, our lips meeting like they've been withering away in the time they've been apart.

It scares me how accurate that feels. And not just since we first kissed. I'm kicking myself for being in John Beecher's orbit for two years, but not making a point to meet him.

Now that our planets have collided, we're determined

to practice what we preach and take advantage of our time together. I straddle him, cradling his flushed cheeks and sliding my tongue against his. Even in the snow, our bodies are burning up. John gently bites my bottom lip, and I moan, grinding over his hardening length through his already tight pants.

"I didn't think there was a downside to skinny jeans," he muses, placing hot kisses down my throat, "until I desperately want you to take them off."

John being so forward makes me want to match his boldness. "I bet I don't need to do that to get you to unravel. What would you be doing if you were the one in charge?"

Competition flashes in his eyes, and in one swift movement, he flips me over and pins me down, erection digging into my inner thigh. "I'd tell you to assume the position."

He slides my legs apart before raising my arms above my head. It dawns on me that we're mirroring the same shapes we were making earlier. I had no idea Snow Gandalfs could be so seductive. "And then what?" I whisper.

Holding eye contact, John slowly thrusts his pelvis against mine, and despite the layers of clothing between us, I can feel every delicious inch. "I'd keep you nice and open like this for me. And I wouldn't stop until I find out the sounds you make when you come."

Merry fucking Christmas to me. I yank John down and kiss him hard, relishing the sweet friction rubbing against my clit. He grips my hips, grounding as deep as he's physically able.

In my lustful haze, I briefly consider the risky situation we've put ourselves in. The sun is about to set, and so far the guests have been content to stay inside, drinking by the fireplace, but it would only take one staff member to come looking for me. We're not deep in the forest; we're next to the fire pits, practically fornicating in public.

And yet. That's not enough for me to slam the brakes. Not when it feels this fucking good. I can only imagine how feral I'll be when he's inside me.

We're working ourselves into a frenzy, throwing caution to the frigid wind, panting until our breath becomes intermingled in a foggy mist. And then John snakes his hands underneath my top layers, bra included, and cups my breasts. My nipples could already cut glass, but when he brushes his thumbs across them, I arch into his cool touch.

"More," I whimper. John pinches and rolls my nipples, all while continuing his thrusts and grazing my earlobe with his teeth.

"Come on, Summer. If I'm going to cream my pants, the least you can do is join me."

The thought sends me over the edge, and I cry out as my climax hits me. John thrusts again, groaning through gritted teeth, holding my hips tight until we stop twitching. When I open my eyes, he's peering down with a joy that's as light and airy as our exhales.

"I don't think there are any holiday traditions that could compete with that," John says, brushing my slightly disheveled hair back. "If I lose feeling in my extremities for being out in the freezing cold, it will have been worth it."

I kiss his icy nose, noticing up close that it's crooked like it's been broken before. Perhaps that's what John was alluding to when he mentioned his accident?

After such a blissful break, though, asking him about it would most certainly kill the mood. And I'd much rather warm up for round two in a claw-footed tub. "You know, I still have Tania's honeymoon suite reserved. With the roads closed today, it would be a shame for the room to go unused."

Whatever guilt John had about stealing his sister's suite disappears as fast as the warmth we generated with our hookup. Shaking off a shiver, he scrambles to his feet, pulling me up with him.

"Might as well," he says with a conspiratorial grin. "I got to change out of these pants anyway. Let's just say the snow isn't the only thing that's made them soaked."

I laugh, dropping my gaze with embarrassment. Who am I? I've only had a handful of mediocre dates in the past twelve years, and now I'm doing the dirty in the dirt. Our Snow Gandalfs have turned into a big blob like they were crushed by the Balrog. Desecrating them was thrilling and unnerving, which is how I feel about John. With his cherry-red hair and facial hardware, he's eerily like Ryan—the kind of guy I could never bring home to my family but who makes me happier than I feel climbing the big walls of Yosemite. I've been dead inside for so long, but in just a few days, John Beecher has brought me back to life.

We pocket the speaker and race to the back entrance. But when John holds the door open for me, I immediately know something's wrong. The lobby is dark save for the natural light streaming through the windows and the candles that have been lit.

"There you are, Summer!" an out-of-breath staff member exclaims. "We've been looking everywhere for you. The power's gone out."

chapter
six

There goes my plan to fuck off the rest of the day and get fucked in one of the most luxurious locations in the valley.

We don't have much time to fix this power problem before the sun fully sets. Since the backup generator is closest to my cabin, it's my responsibility when an issue arises. I even had an electrician give me a crash course for times like these where the roads are obstructed and the pros can't get through.

While I wait for John to discreetly change his pants, I grab a walkie-talkie and lantern, while walking through the game plan with my team. Once he returns and everyone is clear on their instructions, the two of us set off.

Tania and I initially butted heads for many reasons, but one of them was her inability to see why anyone would want to live in the wilderness. Before she fell in love with Nolan, she would have been satisfied staying at Granite Grove and never venturing outside. But what she quickly learned—in part, thanks to me—is that Yosemite isn't your average forest. It's one of the most majestic national parks on earth. People from all over the world would kill to live in the valley and wake up to El Cap and Half Dome every single day. Sure, a park ranger's salary can't compete with what she was earning in tech. But what Tania didn't know was that jobs here are way more competitive than she would expect.

When people would give their nondominant limb to live here, the one thing they willingly accept is bare-bones housing. There aren't that many employers in the park; if you don't work for the National Park Service directly, you're with one of the nature conservancy nonprofits or you work in hospitality, like me.

Housing is hard to come by, and amenities are sparse no matter your job. In what we call Canvas Valley, employees live in tent cabins, made out of the fabric which gave the community its name.

"Where I live in Lost Arrow Spire with the other hospitality workers," I tell John, explaining the nuances of Yosemite housing assignments, "we get slightly upgraded cabins called WOBs."

"Wobs?" John repeats, not catching the acronym.

"Stands for Without Bathrooms. They're hard-sided cabins that come with a couple of twin beds and dressers, so they're better than the tents, but we have shared bathrooms and kitchens. I've been working here long enough that I've got my own AC unit too, but those aren't a given despite how hot it can get in the summer."

John's not used to traveling through snow on foot, and I have to slow my pace so he can keep up with me. "You said more than one bed? Do you have a roommate?"

A pang hits my chest, but I power through. I don't get asked much about life in Yosemite, since everyone I know also lives here, but it's good practice to talk about my past.

"I did. It was Ryan. It's hard to get housing with a partner, especially if they don't work in the same organization, but Ryan was so excited to upgrade from living with Nolan in his van that I couldn't help sneaking him into my cabin. I kept worrying someone would rat us out, but as you know, the Wells brothers were rock climbing royalty. Nobody would dare narc on our local heroes. When news of Ryan's death broke, it's like the whole valley unanimously decided I had been through enough. Granite Grove never assigned me a roommate afterward, and I've been living by myself ever since."

Our conversation gets cut short when the backup generator comes into view, and we make quick work of restoring the power. John holds the lantern for me as I flip the right switches, and I'm glad we brought it, because by the time I complete the order of operations, it's getting dark.

I pull out the walkie-talkie to close the loop. "Come in," I say, speaking to my front desk team on the other end. "We should be good to go, so try resetting the system."

We hear the relieved cheers before the confirmation itself. "That's it! You did it. Oh my goodness, Summer, thank you so much. You saved the day."

I chuckle. "Does that mean I can clock out now?"

"You've earned it—see you tomorrow." The connection clicks off, leaving us on our own. It's not actively snowing, but walking back to the lodge in the pitch black is less appealing when we're steps away from my cabin.

"Do you want to stay at my place tonight? It's not as nice as the honeymoon suite, obviously, but it's got a cozy charm."

John lifts his shoulder, gesturing to the backpack he's carrying. "Like I said before, I usually avoid leaving my house if I can help it, so when I do go outside, I come prepared. Packed all the essentials—pajamas and another set of clothes, toothbrush, and um, some extra protection if we want to pick up where we left off."

"You brought condoms?" I'm glad John thought ahead because I definitely would not have any at my cabin. My perpetual singlehood never bothered me before, but now that I'm brushing the dust off my dating life, it will be an adjustment.

I make a mental note to schedule an appointment with my gynecologist to get back on birth control, before leading the way to Lost Arrow Spire. With the subtle scent of patchouli in the air, the campsite is like a hippie frat party, especially when it's inhabited by mostly young guys who chose the dirtbag life because they equate the corporate nine-to-five with torture. More sophisticated, bougie types like Tania probably think I'm nuts for willingly roughing it with these mountain men, but I've become a proud mountain woman. There's nothing I love more than exploring new terrain and pushing myself to my limit with a gnarly climb. I can feel Ryan's free spirit here, see it in each of my neighbors. We share the same deep-seated sense that Yosemite is home.

John and I head to the communal kitchen first to whip up a quick dinner—grilled cheese sandwiches and canned tomato soup to warm our bellies after weathering the wintry evening. While the sandwiches are toasting, every scruffy dude in a beanie introduces himself to John. I can tell he gets nervous in social situations, so I'm glad everybody makes him feel welcome—even if they give me a knowing glance or an elbow nudge when he's not looking. They've never seen me bring another man around, so I know word will be spreading through the campsite tonight.

Women get a bad rap for being gossipy, but there's no rumor mill like cramped quarters with park employees who have been cooped up during a snowstorm.

After drinking beers with the guys, we take two bottles to go, ready to call it a night. John sticks both drinks in his pockets, so he can take my hand in his while I hold the lantern, directing us back to my cabin.

"It's not much," I warn as I open the door and usher him inside. I haven't had any overnight visitors, so I'm uneasy seeing the interior through his eyes. The two tiny beds pushed together, flanked by worn-down dressers on each side. There are no closets, just a hanging rack in the corner where I keep a very minimalist wardrobe.

That's when I remember that my belongings aren't the only things I'm holding onto. As John traverses the cabin in a few steps, relics from my past life are impossible to ignore: the photos of me and Ryan sitting atop his dresser, which is stuffed with all his clothes I couldn't bear to part with. I used to open the drawers just to inhale his scent, but that has dissipated in the years since. Now that corner of artifacts serves as a shrine, collecting dust and getting eaten by moths.

"Sorry," I say, apologizing before I know why. "I, uh, haven't changed much. I get it if you're not interested in sleeping in a depressing time capsule."

John stares back at me, flummoxed. "Summer, I'm not going anywhere. I'm honored you would open your home to me, and you're entitled to hold onto your memories however you see fit. A late boyfriend isn't the same as an ex-boyfriend, and it would be weird as hell if I got jealous over a few photographs."

He pulls me into his arms. "What I'm more concerned about is that you called where you live a depressing time capsule. I won't pretend to know what Ryan was like, but I'd have to imagine he would want your space to bring you joy—to make room for new hopes and dreams."

I hug John tighter, tears welling as I let his words in. He's right. At first, I thought getting rid of Ryan's stuff would be betraying him and his memory. When Granite Grove never assigned me a roommate, I didn't see the point of downsizing. If I didn't have to share my space with anybody, why not keep the corner the way it was? It seemed better than the alternative at the time, which would be staring at a blank and empty space.

But the emptiness was inside me all along. By refusing to clear out the stuff Ryan no longer needed, I've been unable to truly move on.

I don't believe Ryan is watching me from above or anything, but I can hear him now: *Babe, I'm flattered that you miss me so much and shit, but it's becoming a major bummer. Now pass me that brewski, will ya?*

I smile at the thought. "Honestly, Ryan would be drinking from my beer and talking your ear off. When he and Nolan were together—which, let's face it, was always— I could barely get a word in."

We remove the caps and cheers. At least living in an icebox during the winter keeps your beer cold. "Ryan seems like a good dude," he says.

It's subtle, but I appreciate John using the present tense, even though Ryan's no longer here. I don't go around delusionally correcting people's grammar or anything, pretending he just stepped outside to grab the mail and never came back. But death doesn't erase a person's goodness. "He'd say the same about you. I may not have much dating experience, but I am glad that we finally met. Makes me feel lucky, like I'm going two-for-two."

The cabin doesn't have room for seating, so we kick off our boots and prop ourselves up on my bed. John picks at a thread on his jacket, leaning his ankle against mine. It's as if he has to be touching me in any way he can. "That's a better record than I have," he admits, setting our empty beer bottles on my dresser. "The pants I was wearing earlier have gotten more action than I have in years."

My mind flashes back to our very private—although technically in public—moment. Snowflakes had floated down onto the crook of John's nose, a crook that is more obvious now that we're shoulder to shoulder.

"You don't have to go into it if you don't want to, but you mentioned becoming agoraphobic after an accident. It would be nice to know I'm not the only one that life decided to throw around for no reason."

John grimaces, and I immediately regret springing the topic on him. "No, it's not you," he explains, taking in my stricken face. "It's just I wouldn't characterize myself as an unwitting victim. Ryan's death was a tragedy no one could have prevented. I, on the other hand . . . I got into a car accident when I was in college. I was driving down some winding roads through the foothills to visit a friend, between here and Fresno. I wasn't paying close attention, and I didn't see them coming. Turned left and ran straight into a family's minivan. The only reason I'm not dead is because my old Monte Carlo had such a long hood. It collapsed like an accordion, and the rear-view mirror popped off and broke my nose, but the car absorbed most of the impact, and I was able to walk free."

"And the family?" I grit my teeth, afraid of his answer.

"They were all fine, thank goodness. A little battered and bruised, but I was the one at the two-way stop who jumped the gun. It was my fault they plowed into me.

When a pregnant woman stumbled out of the middle seat, I went completely white. I was so terrified of causing her to miscarriage that I hounded my lawyer for news until he confirmed that both mother and baby were safe."

I let out a breath, putting two and two together. "So that's why it's hard for you to leave your house. You're afraid of getting in another car accident."

John nods. "I'm low-level anxious in most public situations, but driving is the worst. My biggest fear is harming someone again because of a mistake I made. I've been working hard in therapy to improve my coping skills, because it's not feasible to rely on other people for transportation, but it's been a journey. It's a struggle when you don't live in a walkable city. I had no idea that agoraphobia and driving avoidance went hand in hand until I found myself staying home just so I wouldn't have to get behind the wheel. Even now, if I can get something delivered to my front door, I will."

"Healing doesn't have a timeline," I say, reaching for his hand. "Give yourself credit for the progress you've made. The fact that you drove through Yosemite by yourself—in the snow, no less—for this event is a major win."

He squeezes my fingers. "Thank you for saying that. It took me twice as long as it should have because I was fucking petrified, but I made it. And I'm glad I did. At first, I didn't want to disappoint you and the team, but now, I can't imagine bailing and missing this chance to be with you."

He tips my chin, kissing me with a tenderness that would have knocked me off my feet if I wasn't already lying down. It's such a natural and foreign sensation at the same time. On one hand, it feels like we've been together for much longer than a few days. With what we've overcome in our lives, we speak the same language, accented by sorrow and grief. It's comforting to finally be able to share that part of myself with someone who cares for me the way I care for him.

What's not comforting, though, is knowing it won't last. When I first invited John inside, I assumed hooking up with him here would be difficult because of Ryan's lingering presence.

But as John's tongue slips past mine, and the heat between us begins to reignite, it's not the weathered photos in my field of vision dampening the mood.

I never thought anything could be more painful than a loved one passing away, until I'm confronted with the inevitability of losing someone I love who's alive and well.

The admission to myself—that I'm falling for John Beecher, and I can't handle him leaving in less than three days—is what forces me to slow down.

"As much as I want to," I say, pulling away and already missing his taste, "I don't think I'm ready." Not ready to fall in love. Not ready to say goodbye and sink back down into the pit of despair that's been my closest companion until now.

Of course, I don't admit that, so John assumes I'm merely talking about sex. He takes what he considers a temporary rejection in stride.

"We've got all the time in the world." He kisses my forehead as if he's not checking out of Granite Grove as soon as the Merry Masquerade is over. "Plus, there's one thing I miss more than sleeping with a woman."

"Oh yeah? What's that?"

John wraps his arm around my waist and assumes the big spoon position. "*Actually* sleeping together. You don't realize you're touch-starved until you're dying to cuddle."

He makes a good point. Normally, I would insist on completing my nighttime routine, but when I'm cocooned in his warm embrace, the last thing I want to do is hike to the communal bathroom so I can wash my face and brush my teeth.

I smile, eyelids drooping with drowsiness. John mainlines Mountain Dew. A little morning breath won't bother him.

chapter
seven

The next morning, I wake up in a better mood than I have in forever. How could I not? With the bright sun beaming through the windows, I already know the worst of the snowstorm is behind us. When I pick up my phone off the nightstand to check the time and weather, I'm relieved to see the roads have been reopened. The Merry Masquerade is tomorrow, and we're finally in the clear.

The real merriment, though, is the warmth of having John wrapped around me. I lean into him, inhaling his woodsy scent, amplified by Yosemite's natural freshness. It felt good to connect with John on a deeper level last night, but perhaps I was too quick to put the kibosh on having a little bedroom fun.

I arch against John, and he instinctively kisses the back of my neck, breathing me in as he awakens. "Mmm . . . I know you want to go slow, Summer, but if you keep stretching like that and rubbing your ass on me, I'm going to make you late for work."

It's a tempting threat. If only I could take him up on it this very moment. But we've got a big day ahead of us. On top of checking the guests in this afternoon, I promised my team I would be all-hands-on-deck for the last day of party prep.

"Gotta admit you are making a solid case for speeding things up," I say, relishing how his hard length digs into my backside. "How about this—the quicker we get through today's to-do list, the faster we can jump back into bed."

He agrees with a strained groan, and on the count of three, we throw off the comforter and shiver in the winter chill. John rubs my arms to expel the goosebumps before sliding down and giving my bum a squeeze. "And the louder you'll be screaming my name," he rumbles with a low voice.

I push him away with a squeal, before I abandon all my plans and risk getting fired. We're both painfully pent-up, but we're going to have to channel our energy into event planning for now.

We race through our getting ready routine, taking showers in the shared bathrooms and throwing on a change of clothes. Then we stop by the Lost Arrow Spire kitchen to eat a quick breakfast and fill up our thermoses with piping-hot coffee. To John's credit, he remembers every-one's names from last night. I thought the other guys would give us a hard time and crack crude jokes about our sleepover, but he fits right in.

Don't get used to it, I tell myself. It's not like he's sticking around.

But I'm determined not to spend these next days moping, not when John's here now. We make the trek to Granite Grove, appreciating the snow-topped mountains underneath the bright, blue sky.

John takes in a bigger breath than he's probably done while stuck at home. "I can't get over how quiet it is here.

It's like the valley has shushed everyone and everything, so it can be worshipped properly."

"That's a great way of putting it. Don't get me wrong —when Yosemite is packed to the brim in the summer, it can feel as chaotic as a theme park. But this time of year brings a serenity I can't find anywhere else. When Ryan passed, I thought the stillness would drive me nuts, leaving me alone with my worst thoughts, but the solitude was free-ing, actually. Who needs church when you can stare at El Cap and get all the answers to the universe you need?"

He holds my hand as we approach the hotel entrance. "For lack of a better word, amen. The captain is the only big man I need in my life."

I smile. I thought as much, until I fell for John. Now I wouldn't mind having another man around. Someone I can wake up with and rejoice in the beautiful day ahead of us.

Or at least that's what this day had in store for us— until one of my staff ruins everything with one sentence: "A pipe burst in the kitchen."

I HAVE FACED a lot of fears living in Yosemite. I have scared off bears trying to ransack our food supply. I have stepped on some nasty spiders when I forgot to properly store my shoes. And I regularly go on climbing expeditions, dangling off cliffs thousands of feet in the air.

But walking into the Granite Grove industrial kitchen is like confronting my worst nightmare.

"We were in the thick of it this morning," the head chef explains. "Balancing the breakfast shift with prepping for tomorrow's party. But the shifting temperatures from this past storm must have done a number on the already ancient plumbing, because all of a sudden, it's like a geyser went off."

No kidding. I can't even tell which station was the original culprit, because a chain reaction must have fucked up multiple sinks. The entire floor is flooded, and the crew is scrambling to contain the damage, using as many towels and buckets as they can get their hands on.

"And the food?" I ask, terrified to learn the extent of this catastrophe.

"Some of it got waterlogged, but most of what was already out was salvageable. That's not what I'm worried about." The chef gestures to the massive refrigerator. "The last thing we need with standing water is an electrical surge, so we've cut off the appliances along with the water supply. We need to store the perishables somewhere else until we can fix the plumbing and dry out the kitchen. Otherwise, the food will spoil. The clock has already started, and we're running out of time."

Tears pinprick the corners of my eyes, and my cheeks overheat with shame. Just when the storm lets up and I think we're in the clear, an absolute disaster happens. There's nothing merry about a masquerade without any food. Granite Grove's event may not be as expensive as the Sentinel House's, but our guests still spent good money and expect to not starve. I can see them now—their angry faces and flood of one-star reviews, calling for my firing for hosting the Fyre Festival of holiday parties.

Hands gripping my shoulders jolt me out of my spiral. "Summer, look at me," John says. "We did not come all this way, conquering closed roads and power outages, to give up now. You have experienced the worst that life has thrown at you, and you came out the other side. And frankly, I did not hyperventilate every mile of this trip to call it quits. If anyone can make it happen, it's us. This doesn't have to be the end."

I choke down a sob. I'm not sure if he recognizes the double meaning in his words, but it's not only the end of the party he's talking about. I realize, deep down, John would never give up on me. Not on the projects we partner on, and not on whatever this relationship is meant to be. I was so ready to walk away from both, retreating into the dark place I've been trapped in, but not if he can help it. I have no idea what this means for us—either in the next few hours or the years ahead—but if John isn't going to throw in the towel, then I don't want to either.

"But how are we going to get out of this mess?" I lament, biting my lip to keep it from wobbling. "And don't give me some bullshit about Christmas miracles. We're as likely to witness divine intervention as we are to see Santa coming down the chimney."

John squeezes my shoulder again. "You don't have to believe in a higher power to have faith. Do you trust your team to come through? Do you trust me?"

"Yes," I say without hesitation. Belonging to a religion that preached platitudes when I needed support the most did not bring me peace. I'm better off without a god that only took from me—my autonomy, my sanity, my first love. But when I stare at the flesh and blood in this kitchen, John and the culinary staff aren't imaginary. They're real and they're right here, prepared to give everything they've got.

John smiles, mischief tugging on the corners on his mouth. I gotta say, his determination is infectious. "That's the Christmas spirit," he says. "Let's fucking do this."

chapter
eight

After deliberating with the team over our options and vetoing a suggestion to ask for help from the Sentinel House—I don't care if it *is* the giving season—we come up with the most palatable solution. Between the Village Store and the various employee communal kitchens, we should have enough fridge space to store food for four hundred guests. Fingers crossed that Granite Grove can fix its plumbing and get its appliances back up and running, but until then, we won't have to worry about the whole meal spoiling. It's not a perfect plan, but it saves me from having to put my tail between my legs and admit that Sentinel is superior.

John pulls aside a few volunteers. "Most of the crew has to stay back to finish out the breakfast and lunch shifts," he explains. "But if the rest of us pack our vehicles to the brim with food and split up, we can beat this game of fridge Tetris. I once fit a month's worth of Mountain Dew while making room for real sustenance, so I'm confident this can work."

I have to hold down the front desk, so I have no choice

but to have hope that everything will go alright. "Be careful out there," I tell John. "The storm may be over, but the conditions can be just as dangerous when the temperatures rise. The snow turns into what we call Sierra cement. It can become so heavy and wet that it knocks down trees and collapses roofs. At least it's cold enough outside that the food should survive the trip. Just go slow and get there in one piece."

Flashbacks from the Matterhorn threaten to cloud my vision, and I have to remember to breathe from my diaphragm to steady myself. Driving to the Village Store isn't as risky as climbing one of the world's most treacherous peaks, and I refuse to entertain John meeting the same fate as Ryan.

"I'll come back to you. I promise." He kisses my forehead, and I'm tempted to say the words that are on the tip of my tongue, to tell John I love him. But whether it's apprehension that we've only known each other for four days or superstition that I'll jinx John into a terrible accident, I hold back. I have to believe him when he says we have all the time in the world.

I spend the morning impatiently waiting for an update from John, rapping my knuckles on the counter while checking out the last of the guests. Why anyone would choose to spend the holidays at home instead of the most enchanting valley on earth is beyond me, but I'm relieved when I'm finally able to get away from the front desk. Just as I'm about to call John's cell, two unlikely arrivals walk through the entrance.

"You made it!" I rush to give Nolan and Tania a group

hug until I remember why they're late in the first place. "I thought you'd be stuck at home recuperating."

Nolan slides up his pant leg to show off his ankle brace. "We went to urgent care to be safe, but it wasn't as bad as the last time I took a tumble. No crutches this time."

His wife gives him side-eye. "So now we both have rules. I will never use my phone while belaying, and Nolan is not allowed to free solo the house to put up Christmas lights."

I chuckle. Their relationship has been a little rough-and-tumble, literally, but they're the perfect match, overcoming every obstacle thrown their way.

"I'm so glad you were able to make it in time for the Merry Masquerade." I check my watch, which reads noon. "Have you eaten lunch yet? We had quite the kitchen kerfuffle this morning, but it sounds like our chefs have been able to work things out."

Nolan shakes his head. "Nah, we're good, thanks. Tania was feeling nostalgic, so we decided to pick up some groceries at the Village Store and cook in the van. I promised her I'd make her my special vegan mac and cheese, for old time's sake."

I'd be overcome with their cuteness if I wasn't distracted by the mention. "The Village Store? That's where John was headed to preserve the food for the party after our plumbing went on the fritz. You didn't see him?"

Tania's brow furrows. "No, he wasn't there. And we would know, because I wandered every single aisle to make sure we didn't forget anything."

I check my watch again. It's been hours. Even if John drove glacially slow and stocked every shelf in the store's fridges by himself, he should be done by now. And if he wasn't shooting the shit with his sister and brother-in-law, he should be here, awaiting my lunch break so we can congratulate ourselves on saving the day once again.

I hurry out the entrance, Tania at my heels and Nolan hobbling after. Craning my head, I scan the parking lot, but there's no sign of John's car.

Tania echoes my racing thoughts. "If he's not here or at the store, where could he be?" She walks in circles, as if she expects John to jump through the trees as some kind of sick prank. "Summer, he's terrified of driving. He got into this bad accident when he was in college, and it's taken years for him to get behind the wheel again—"

"I know," I say, cutting her off. "He told me everything. We've gotten really close, actually . . . " I trail off as Tania's blinks in surprise. This isn't the most appropriate moment to tell her that I'm dating her brother, not when we have no idea where he is. Bringing Tania up to speed will have to wait. We need to find John before—before it's too late.

Panic bubbles up my throat at the thought, making it hard to breathe. The same fear I felt when I heard about Nolan's fall threatens to paralyze me again, and this time, John isn't here to bring me back to earth.

I can't lose another person I love. *I can't.*

"We're going to find him," Nolan insists, as he rubs Tania's arm to comfort her. He turns toward me. "Between the two of us, there isn't an inch of this park we don't know." He springs into action, pulling out his phone to alert his climbing friends. I shoot a message of my own to my front desk team, so they know our plans and can sit tight in case we need to call search-and-rescue. If I could pick one thing I love most about working in Yosemite, it's that we have each other's backs, no matter what.

I try calling and texting John multiple times, but when the messages don't deliver, it confirms my suspicions that wherever he is has spotty connection. That doesn't really narrow down possible locations because that's just a fact of life in a national park.

We jump in the van. I offer to drive since Nolan's got a bum ankle, and Tania doesn't know the roads here like I do. Thankfully, there are only so many routes to get around the valley, and driving the full loop takes about thirty minutes, absent of traffic and bad weather. We take the most direct path to the Village Store, following the route John must have driven.

Sure enough, halfway to our destination, we see John's car on the side of the road, intact and undisturbed. Images of crushed metal wrapped around a tree vanish the moment I see the driver door open and see the top of his cherry-red hair.

"John!" I shout, tumbling out of the van. I barrel toward him as fast as I can, nearly wiping out in the snow. He catches me as I make impact, and I squeeze the air from his lungs. Out of the corner of my eye, I see Tania and Nolan exchange bemused looks. So much for keeping our dating on the down-low.

"I'm fine," he gasps as I loosen my grip. "I just hit a pothole and got a flat tire. There's no cell service out here, and although I could have probably walked the rest of the way to the store, I didn't want to risk getting lost and making things worse." He gestures to the trunk of his car. "Most of the food should be safe, but some of the shellfish may be questionable after all this time, even in a cooler in the middle of winter. I'm sorry."

I pull back. "Sorry? What do you have to be sorry for?"

The wind picks up, and John smooths my hair without a second thought. "Because I'm supposed to be prepared for anything, and I don't even have a spare tire. Because you've been working so damn hard to plan the perfect holiday party, and I didn't want one more thing to go wrong. I didn't want to disappoint you."

I take his face in my hands. "Fuck the party. None of that matters if something terrible happens to you. I hate sounding like a broken record, but I would know. Even the best-made plans can fall apart in an instant. Someone could be at fault, or no one could be—we have no control. I learned life can throw you a rock to the skull and it's game over. Just like that." I snap my fingers. "There is no fate or predestination or divine will. There's only chaos. We get one life, and I can't believe it took a flat tire to get me to see things so clearly." I take a breath, lest I run out of steam before I get the words out. "I love you, John. I know that sounds outrageous since we just met, but—"

John collides into me, capturing my lips in a kiss and scooping me up for a spin around in the snow. Immediately, I feel lighter in a way that has nothing to do with being temporarily airborne. After experiencing such tragedy, I lost hope in happy endings. Now my heart is soaring because I have the chance to write one with him.

"In case it wasn't obvious," he says as he sets me down, "I love you too. An embarrassing amount. I knew as soon as I saw you that you're my Summer. You bring out the sun on the cloudiest days." I can tell he can't believe his luck either. Maybe that's the real Christmas miracle. It has nothing to do with frankincense and myrrh. It's the fact that out of all the holiday parties in all the world, we happened to plan this one together.

"Ahem." We turn toward the throat clearing to see Tania and Nolan cheezing at us. John's sister gestures to the van. "You wanna take your makeout sesh on the road? I'm freezing my ass off here."

Right. I'm glad they're both so casually supportive of us, but we're not out of the literal woods yet. We've got a celebration to finish before we can celebrate what comes next.

Using the mobile hotspot in his van, Nolan directs his climbing search party to bring a spare tire, while Tania helps us to get the food inside so we can complete our mission.

"Alright, let's get a move on," Nolan says, settling in the passenger seat.

John looks back at his car. "Don't we need to wait until your friends arrive so we can direct them to the right location?"

"Nah. Anyone who free solos in Yosemite can find a pinky-sized hold on a giant wall of granite, so this will be a piece of cake for them. I dropped a pin of the car's coordinates and left the keys in it unlocked. They'll have the tire replaced and meet us at the Village Store in no time."

As much as I appreciate that Nolan's buddies can come through for us, the busted tire is not our only problem. "And what about the spoiled seafood? Or Granite Grove's busted kitchen?"

Soon, we arrive at the store, and Tania pulls out her phone as soon as the van is in park. "You've got fire pits, right?" she says. "We just have to get creative. And I know the perfect chef who can help."

chapter
nine

Usually, I'm so burnt out from work this time of year that I'm ready for the holidays to be over as quickly as possible. Guests would always lament when we took the Christmas decor down, and there I'd be, looking forward to the stark, cold emptiness of January when all the pomp and circumstance disappeared. If I was going to be miserable on the inside, I wanted the outside to match.

This year is different. In less than a week, John changed my entire outlook on the calendar. Funny how you're ready to seize the day—any day—when you have someone by your side who energizes you like a shot of Mountain Dew straight to the veins.

Tonight, however, my drink of choice is a well-deserved glass of champagne. The final preparations went smoothly as they could have. Tania's childhood friend and favorite chef Vahe Derderian was already in Fresno with his family, so he and his girlfriend offered to fill his truck with firewood, skewers, cast-iron cookware, and other essential equipment so they could help the culinary team grill meat and veggie kebabs in the fire pits. They were so delicious that nobody missed the shrimp scampi we had planned on. Vahe even dressed up like Santa and brought s'mores ingredients to turn the outdoor patio into a family-friendly affair.

Inside the decked-out ballroom, though, is a romantic sight to behold. After Nolan's free solo friends repaired John's flat tire and drove his car back to the lodge, they offered to take our decorations to new heights. In record time, they scaled the walls—literally—and installed strings of twinkle lights and sparkling snowflakes, so it looks like snow is falling from the vaulted ceiling.

"I didn't think any party could rival the grandeur of Yosemite," says Nolan as he follows my gaze upward, "but damn if this doesn't come close." He clinks his glass against mine. "Congrats, Summer. Ryan would be so happy for you."

I brush off the praise. "I didn't plan this event by myself. It was definitely a team effort."

"Led by you and your dogged determination, but that's not what I'm talking about. He'd be glad you found a plus-one worth celebrating with."

"You think so?" I take a self-conscious sip. "I've avoided dating for so long that it's hard not to feel guilty. We may not believe Ryan is staring down from the afterlife, but I would never want him to think I'd forget about him."

"You never will, and more importantly, John wouldn't let you. I've got to know him better through Tania, so I mean it when I say he's a good guy. He wants to be involved in every part of your life, even the parts that hurt the most. It took me forever to figure it out for myself, but falling in love makes those parts hurt less. Makes those mountains easier to climb." He lets out a breath, the ache of loss getting to him too. "And if there's one thing I know about my brother, he would never want you to stop climbing. We all need a belayer, Summer. He would be stoked you found one as rad as John."

Phew. I fan my face, willing the waterworks to stay back. The only tears I want to cry tonight are happy ones, which means I need to find said plus-one, pronto. "Where is John anyway? I know the party just got started, but he's not the type to be fashionably late."

Nolan drains the rest of his champagne. "Like me, he doesn't attend fancy shindigs often, so Tania's helping him put his tie on properly. Here he comes!"

I face the entrance, and even in the dim lighting, the sight of John Beecher in a fitted suit nearly knocks me over. We didn't coordinate outfits, but I have to laugh at the coincidence. Whereas I went with a ruby-red strapless gown, he's wearing a deep emerald tuxedo. We're like an issue of *Vanity Fair*, Christmas edition. So why do I feel like there's something missing . . . ?

The realization hits me as John approaches. "Shoot—I forgot to grab our masks! How can I be hosting a merry masquerade when I'm not on theme?" I turn to ask Nolan to fetch them, but he's already slipped away to dance with his wife, bum ankle be damned. I admire that level of devotion.

John takes my hand, leading me to the dance floor. "The masks are cool, but if it's alright with you, I'd rather stare at your gorgeous face. You look stunning, Summer."

I appreciate his compliment, but I'm grateful that, for once, I feel as good as I look. I could never shake off this cloud of grief before, and I'm ready for the sun to come out so I can bask in this glow.

The jazz band I hired has created a romantic ambience, playing slow ballads we can easily sway to. And if I'm not mistaken, Vahe's girlfriend Tori has squeezed in at the piano for a guest performance. It's what I love most about Yosemite—it brings people together from all walks of life.

Like me and John. Despite what has been taken from us, I know this valley will give us everything we could possibly want and more.

"So . . . " I say, "I know we entered this relationship at lightning speed, but we can take our time. I'm used to living on my own, so please don't feel pressured to relocate. Granite Grove would love to have you host more paint-and-sips whenever you visit."

John cocks his head. "Visit? Oh, I'm not making that treacherous drive on a regular basis. I know I made it sound like I'm trapped inside at all times, but I also genuinely like being a homebody. It's been a dream of mine to live in a cabin in the woods. I have to figure out a way to get better bandwidth out here, so I can do my design work and pwn newbs on my PC, but until then, the business center here will do. So you better accept my roommate application because I'm not going anywhere. Tania's already warned me that you're going to teach me to climb and start dragging me up mountains, but that's fine by me if you don't mind driving." His expression softens. "As long as I'm by your side, I'm down for any adventure."

I beam, my brain whirring with the trips we can take once the weather warms up. "There are so many places I wanna take you. Seeing the giant sequoias in Mariposa Grove, floating down the Merced River, hanging out at Hetch Hetchy. I can't wait to show you around the park!"

John smiles. "Me too, but let's take it one day at a time." The music transitions into a sultrier tune. "One *night* at a time."

When his hands slide down my hips and drift toward

my ass, I get the hint. In my giddiness over my favorite Yosemite spots, I forgot about the fun we can continue having once the sun sets. "What did you have in mind for tonight?"

He pulls me in closer, his gaze falling to the tops of my breasts. "I thought I'd have to bribe my sister for the honeymoon suite, but she handed over her key without a problem. Said she and Nolan were staying in his van like they did when they first met, so she was more than happy to give us a Christmas Eve to remember. I say we let her handle the rest of the evening while we go throw ourselves a more intimate party."

"You don't have to tell me twice." I lead him out of the ballroom, excited to make Santa's naughty list this year.

chapter
ten

We take our tongues out of each other's mouths long enough to open the door to the honeymoon suite and tumble inside. The interior is much larger than our standard rooms but embodies the same woodland aesthetic—with the added bonus of a cozy electric fireplace and a claw-footed tub for two.

"So much room for activities!" I exclaim before I can stop myself, but thankfully, John laughs at the *Step Brothers* reference.

"Did we just become best friends?" he says with a wry smile.

"Yup. Best friends, belayers, plus-ones, party hosts, partners in crime, boyfriend and girlfriend. Lovers." I turn around so John can unzip my gown, and he gladly obliges.

"Mmm . . . I like the sound of that last one. But you can call me anything you like if I can strip you naked every night."

"Then it's a good thing I didn't wear any underwear." I step out of the dress and let it fall to the floor along with

John's slack jaw. "So what will our first activity be—fireplace fun or bubble bath?"

"Getting clean after getting dirty makes the most sense, but the truth is I need to have you on the closest surface possible." He removes his tie and unbuttons his shirt and pants like his life depends on it. "If I have to take one step before touching you, I will explode."

With that, he pulls me down to the faux fur rug in front of the fireplace, somehow ripping off his clothes on the way down.

In an instant, we're skin to skin, and I'm overwhelmed by how much there is to explore. Most guys working in Yosemite have a tattoo here and there—unless they're one of those crunchy granola, body-is-a-temple types—but I've never hooked up with one with ink covering every square inch below his neck. It's clear John treats his skin like yet another canvas, showcasing an eclectic collection of patchwork-styled pieces. I roll on top of him so I can trace them, admiring his favorite things: video game emblems, anime characters, and yes, even a 'Baja Be Thy Blast' tribute to his beloved drink.

"Summer, I appreciate how much you love looking at my art, but this is definitely one of those situations where touching is encouraged. So get your ass over here and sit on my face if you're gonna ogle the goods."

When you put it that way . . . there's something so attractive when someone comes out of their shell. With a strength I didn't know he had, John grips my hips to turn me around reverse cowgirl and pull me toward his waiting mouth.

It's not a position I've ever tried—I'm too afraid of suffocating a poor man in the throes of ecstasy—but John's eagerness overcomes my anxiety. Between his tongue circling my clit and his nose stud adding extra sensation, he's making a solid case for risk-taking.

"Remember," he pants between my thighs, "there's no heaven. We only get one life, and if this is how mine ends, so be it. I can't think of a better way to go."

He yanks me closer, and the momentum causes me to make contact with the one body part of his that isn't tatted or pierced. Thanks to my above-average height and his above-average cock, we can taste each other at the same time.

The moment I take him in my mouth, he moans, increasing the tempo. I cry out, realizing that I'm a terrible multitasker when every lick and bite sends me into a tailspin.

"That's it," he praises. "I'll get mine, don't you worry. Just sit back and come for me."

The closer I get to climaxing, the rougher I grind against him, stroking his dick to match my thrusts. The fire flickering in the dimly lit room can't compete with the one burning inside me, and with a few more pumps, those embers ignite into an inferno.

"Ohhhh *fuck*. Right there. Holy—" The pressure snaps, and John has to hold me in place, so I don't slide off him. He lets me ride out my orgasm, my legs shaking, until I'm able to catch my breath. But not a second longer.

"What are you doing?" I gasp as my racing heartbeat comes down. John licks his lips, wiping my excess slickness off his chin, which would be hot as hell if I wasn't distracted by what he's holding.

"I told you I was gonna get mine," he says, lifting up his necktie. "If you're on board with it."

My heart revs back up in the best way. Is it irrational for us to jump straight to light bondage for our first time? Sure, but we confessed our love for each other days after meeting. I'm starting to think rational is overrated. If John Beecher is going to be down for any adventure I take him on, then I can repay the favor.

I offer him my wrists. "Take it all and then some."

With the kind of deftness and precision that can only come from painting masterpieces, John maneuvers me onto my knees and secures my wrists with his tie behind my back, leaving the tail loose. At first, I wonder how I'm going to balance when I can't support myself on all fours, until he pulls on the end, which keeps me suspended.

Unlike me, John's an excellent multitasker, rendering me immobile while fishing a condom out of his pants on the floor. In a few quick moves, he rips the foil wrapper open and slides the protection down his cock, standing at attention.

"I can feel your wetness leaking down your legs. Is that from riding my face, or are you that desperate to get railed ass-up on this rug?"

"Both," I whimper. "Please, John. I've been pent up for days, and I can't take it anymore."

When he pushes in from behind, one glorious inch at a time, I realize I miscalculated. Yes, I've wanted to jump his bones since I met him five days ago. But as he fills me up, he's eliminating an emptiness I've felt for over a decade.

Back in my cabin, when I wasn't ready to take our relationship to the next level, moving on felt morally wrong, a betrayal of my love for Ryan. But now that my love has expanded to include John, that guilt has subsided. I knew Ryan better than anyone, and he wasn't the jealous type. He'd be proud I'm finally getting fucked properly again.

"You still with me?" John pauses, sensing a shift in the air. It warms my heart that beneath the ink and his nihilistic outlook on life, he's a soft teddy bear. But that's not the animal I need right now.

I look back to make direct eye contact. "Did I tell you to stop?"

His pupils dilate at the taunt, flashing with a competitive streak. "Now you've done it. You're lucky you took Christmas off because you're going to need the entire day to recuperate."

He jerks the tie back, lifting me up as he thrusts with increasing force. I got to hand it to him. Even as our knees are rubbed red from rugburn, he's determined to make me eat my words.

And he succeeds. All I can manage are pants, gasps, grunts, and moans. His free hand palms my breast, pinching my nipple as he kisses the column of my throat.

"You're so close, aren't you?" he whispers in my ear. "I can feel you clenching hard around me. Why don't you give me my Christmas present already and come on my cock?"

John's fingers rub my clit with fervor, not stopping until I'm undone. My inner walls clamp down like a vice, and he lets out a groan, pumping his spend into me. We stay like that, breath ragged and limbs twitching, while John places tender kisses down my spine.

"You know," I say as he unties my wrists, "that was way sweeter than sugar plums or whatever weird treats that Christmas songs are always going on about."

John laughs. "Summer McKenzie, for as long as you'll have me, I promise to be the gift that keeps on giving." He touches his forehead to mine. "I love you."

"I love you too." I indulge in another slow, lingering kiss, grateful to have found my reason for the season. I don't believe in most things, but I believe in us.

All of a sudden, my feet come out from under me as

John scoops me up and pads into the lavish bathroom. "Alright, break's over," he says. "If we're gonna get clean in the tub, I got to get you way, *way* dirtier first."

I squeal with glee, wondering how many surfaces we can desecrate before the clock strikes midnight and we enter a new day—and our new lives—together.

THE END

thank you

Thank you for reading *Love Me Merrily*! It would mean the world if you'd consider writing a review on Amazon and Goodreads, as well as recommending the book on social media. Word of mouth has a huge impact on an author's success, and it helps other readers discover new books to enjoy.

Can't get enough of Summer and John? To gain access to a special bonus epilogue from John's point of view, visit alyssajarrett.com/love-me-merrily

acknowledgments

Since this is my first novella, I'll do my best to keep my thank-yous brief. After all, there are holidays to celebrate!

To my editor Kristen Tate at the Blue Garret. You're forever a member of the Glam Fam as this series would not be the same without you.

To my beta readers Ashley, Brooke, Heather, and Jess. Thank you for always being down to read my latest shenanigans. And a special shout-out to Emily for helping me make life in Yosemite sound as authentic as possible— our national parks are better because of people like you.

To my critique partners and everyone in my inner circle who read early versions of *Love Me Merrily*, including Kel, Lily, Rowan, and Sophia. Even when I say something ridiculous like, "I'm writing an atheist holiday romance with Machine Gun Kelly vibes," you consider that a pro rather than a con.

To my brother and cover designer Nick Jarrett. I gave you a heads up that John was going to sound familiar, so thank you for not being too weirded out by that. I couldn't imagine anyone better to inspire this story, design its stunning cover, and contribute to the book's kickass playlist. Please save some talent for the rest of us.

And, lastly, to my readers. I may not believe in a higher power, but I have faith in you. Thank you for giving me the opportunity to share the stories of my heart. I wish you the merriest time of year, wherever you are.

love on the rocks

a sneak peek

Want to find out how Tania and Nolan fell in love? Please continue reading for an excerpt of Book 2 in the Glam Fam series, *Love on the Rocks*.

chapter
one

Unhappy hour. Drink your feelings hour. C-suite suck-up hour. I'm a marketing executive—shouldn't I be able to come up with better names for this event? All of my colleagues seem to be happy enough. It's the last day of our corporate retreat in Yosemite, and the presentations and brainstorming sessions are finally over.

You should be grateful, Tania Beecher, I keep telling myself. Everything in the bar at the Granite Grove Lodge spells luxury: the historic stone interior with exposed wooden beams along the vaulted ceiling, the warm lighting from elaborate chandeliers, the plush furniture perfectly arranged for cozy conversations.

If I'd stayed in journalism, I'd be in some grimy dive bar, commiserating over the latest round of pink slips at yet another dying newspaper. It took a decade for me to break into the tech industry and claw my way up to vice president of marketing at Habituall, one of Silicon Valley's hottest tech companies. But as I sink deeper into my tufted chair, clutching an exquisitely expensive Napa cabernet, I feel not satisfied, but suffocated.

Everyone on my team is giddy and getting along, clustered together in a boisterous group near the bar—I just can't bring myself to join in the festivities. Harris Shepherd, one of my top content marketers, meets my glance and I quickly look away. Not just because I can't handle chitchat right now—*shit*, he's walking over—but also because his soft, gray eyes are so gorgeous that it's hard to make eye contact.

"You think you got enough there, Tania?" Harris clinks his wine glass against mine, nearly sloshing Silver Oak's finest on the hardwood floor.

Harris has that thirty-something hipster vibe on lock: a dark, full beard and equally thick hair with a silver streak that matches those eyes I have to avoid getting lost in. I cough, as if trying to hack up my lustful thoughts. I'm his boss, for christ's sake. Get it together. "The bartender got generous with the pours. It's not like I asked for a double."

He takes in my nervous laugh. "Maybe you should have a double. It wouldn't kill you to enjoy yourself for once."

"I *am* having fun." I take a defensive gulp of my drink to make my point. "I'm a little stressed over Q1 planning— that's all."

Harris squints his perfect eyes with disapproval. "Come on. That's bullshit, and you know it. I've seen that fifty-slide deck you've been obsessed with. You've had every *i* dotted, *t* crossed, and penny counted since Thanksgiving. There's no way in hell you overlooked anything, and I would bet my Hydrow on it."

Okay, that gets me to laugh for real. Habituall gives every team member a two-hundred-dollar stipend each month to spend on fitness, and I've been approving Harris's expense reports for over a year, so I know exactly how much his rowing machine means to him. And from the way his toned arms bulge in his black Henley when he crosses them, I don't blame him. I remind myself for the hundredth time that he has a girlfriend—whom he met while he was DJ-ing on the weekends, of course.

"The content team's jumping in the hot tub after happy hour if you want to join us. No mentions of AP Style or SEO allowed. Bring your wine, and come unwind."

I should want to say yes. I should want to sit in a hot tub with a ridiculously expensive glass of wine and celebrate our breakneck period of record growth with my team. But the only feeling I can identify is this one:

I don't want to be here anymore.

"Thanks, but you go ahead," I say, passing him my wine glass. "Take that, and don't let it go to waste. I'm going to go for a walk and get some fresh air."

"We're around if you change your mind." He frowns but doesn't press the issue, which makes me think it was a pity invite anyway, then walks off to rejoin the rest of the marketing team.

Although I would describe myself as an "indoor cat," Yosemite in early January is absolutely awe-inspiring: calm and quiet, pristine and pure, ideal for a tightly wound workaholic who has to remember to take a deep breath every now and then. Maybe I haven't spent a single dollar of my fitness stipend, but I can take a stroll in this majestic national park outside. My longtime therapist, Dahlia, suggested I go on a walk to recharge when I texted her earlier today, and for once, I'll be able to tell her I took her advice.

I stride out the door into an Ansel Adams photograph come to life and regret my decision as soon as the icy chill slaps me right in the face.

If I was anywhere else, I would have no problem abandoning my plan and sneaking back up to my room to watch rom-coms instead. But as the sun dips over the mountains, illuminating the peaks in deep orange underneath cotton-candy-streaked skies, I have to admit that it's not just the thirty-degree weather taking my breath away.

It wouldn't kill me to take a walk around and enjoy the view, I think to myself.

Would it though? The little hamster of anxiety in my brain—I call him Hammy—butts in. *You haven't reapplied your sunscreen yet, and just because it's freezing doesn't mean your skin can't get burned in the elements. And you don't even have your trusty water bottle—what if you get lost and die of dehydration?*

Calm down, Hammy. I'm only stretching my legs. You've been doing so many mental laps that I forget I need to move my actual body on occasion.

You sure about that? he insists, his imaginary hamster feet sprinting endlessly on the squeaky wheel in my mind. *You do know you're wearing Ralph Lauren leather riding boots, right? You look like you'd be better off playing polo than going for a hike in the snow.*

I hate when he makes a good point. Lord knows I'm no equestrian—I haven't been around horses since I was a kid living on the outskirts of Fresno, feeding carrots to my neighbor's mares—but I'm even less suited for real winters. I live in the Bay Area, after all, so the only cold-weather attire I own is a stack of corporate-branded Patagonia jackets and the Ted Baker peacoat I'm currently wearing.

It's fine, I keep repeating as I scuffle away from the lodge and down a dirt hiking trail. There's not much snow on the ground, nothing I can't stomp through. Setting my smartwatch to outdoor walk mode, I set off toward the sunset, surprisingly upbeat considering there's no hot cocoa or fireplace in sight. But nothing makes me feel more accomplished than crossing items off my "I really should" list: Visit someplace new? Check. Do some cardio? On it. Connect with nature? Hell yeah.

Look at me, Hammy. All the kids these days talk about touching grass, and I'm out here like a natural adventurer.

I ignore his stubborn squeaks and power through the nerves, enjoying the smell of pine as I breathe deeper than I have in a long time. The muscles in my jaw slowly loosen and my shoulders fall away from my ears.

It occurs to me then that my urge to flee the not-so-happy hour earlier was just Hammy fretting. I'm not having an existential crisis, and I don't need to escape my job. I just need to take that six-week sabbatical I've earned after six years with Habituall. Maybe a few months from now, though—or even next year. It's not like I can peace out after we just got back from winter break—even if I spent most of it working anyway. You can get a lot done when the office shuts down, you know.

I channel Dahlia again and tell myself to stop thinking about work and pay attention to my body. My skin tingling in the cold, my feet moving down the path. The farther I go, the more limber I become, and it's downright thrilling to break out of the sedentary cast my desk job has molded around me. Are these the exercise endorphins everyone's always going on about?

The air stings my lungs and the increasing incline burns my thighs, but I move quickly to keep myself warm, not bothering to keep track of which paths I'm taking as the trail forks off. I resist the urge to pull out my phone and check the same five silly apps, remembering an article I read that explained how our phones had effectively replaced ciga-rettes as our go-to distraction. They give our hands something to do, without the cancer risk. I've felt enough compulsive twitchiness on this work retreat to know that a habit doesn't need nicotine to be addictive.

The sun's in the west, so I keep hiking further and further into the forest, knowing I've got that molten ball in the sky as my compass.

Do you though?

I stop in my tracks, branches snapping ominously under my boots. It's always worse when Hammy whispers instead of squeals. But when I look to my left and no longer see the sun, I realize he's right. Everything is indeed not okay. When I stepped outside, the mountaintops were illuminated like lit cigarettes, but now they're being put out as fast and unceremoniously as butts smashed into an ashtray.

When I pull my phone from my coat pocket and turn on its flashlight, those four trusty bars have disappeared. Meaning I'm by myself, out in the stark wilderness without any cell service, and it's getting colder and darker every second.

Fuck. Fuck fuckity fuck. I whip around, hoping to catch a glimpse of the lodge in the distance, but it must be miles behind me. With the sun officially set, I can't tell east from west, up from down, and it's not like I can get Google Maps to point me in the right direction. How could I be so foolish? Hammy doesn't have to scream to wake me up to the dire circumstances.

It's pitch dark. The flashlight on my phone is rapidly draining my battery. And, worst of all, it starts to snow. At first, there are just a few flakes sparkling in the light from my phone. But after just a minute they're not sparkling as much as settling. Settling in a flurry on my frigid nose, incessantly blinking eyelashes, and gloveless hands. They're conforming to my increasingly damp coat and piling up around my boots—and everywhere else.

The snowfall is heavy enough that the path beneath me has disappeared. I try to double back and return the way I came, but with my footprints getting covered as fast as I'm making them, I can no longer orient myself. Wherever I go, it's white snow on the ground and blackness all around me. I've never experienced the weather take a turn for the worse like this. I mean, climate change is real, but changing this quickly? Fucking unreal.

"Hey!"

Leave me alone, Hammy. I don't have time for this. I need to get back to the lodge before I succumb to exposure. It looks like there's an area up ahead where the trees thin— maybe I can tell where I am from there.

"Stop!"

Absolutely not. That's how hypothermia gets you. You stop moving, and all of a sudden, the warmth of oblivion envelops you before you have a clue what's happening. It's why folks are found frozen in their birthday suits, and I am *not* about to die literally naked and afraid. I keep moving forward up a slight rise. There are definitely fewer trees ahead.

"Can you hear me? I said stop!"

"And I said leave me alone, Hammy!" Wait a minute. I said that out loud, which means I responded to a real person, not my imaginary hamster. I've got a vivid imagination—that's undeniable—but even I stop short of actual hallucinations.

Milliseconds later, an abnormally strong arm pulls me back with so much force that I collide into a sheer wall of muscle.

"I don't know who Hammy is, but if he followed you any further, you'd both be falling down that cliff."

I aim my flashlight in the direction my rescuer is pointing. Just a few paces away, the ground drops off precipitously into a pit of rock and darkness.

I whip back around, and he holds up a hand to shield his eyes from the flashlight. "Do you mind turning that off? I've got it covered."

Quickly tapping the screen, I adjust to my surroundings, settling my gaze on the person in front of me. A man, who looks like he's about my age, with one hand on his headlamp and the other braced against my waist to keep me balanced. Normally, I'd be startled by being held by a stranger, but my body's too frozen in place to step back in surprise.

"Who are you? And why are you out here?" My voice comes out shaky but holds onto its edge, clearly not as comfortable as my extremities to discover a source of warmth in the wild.

"That's supposed to be my line." He chuckles softly, crinkling his eyes and immediately putting me more at ease. His voice is warm and deep, like his embrace shielding me from the snow.

"You didn't answer my question," I project loudly against the wind. My accusatory tone makes me cringe, but he's not at all bothered.

"How about we get you someplace safe before formal introductions, alright?"

He charges down a path leading away from the cliff, but it's difficult for me to keep up. He's properly suited up for snow in several hooded, waterproof jackets and well-worn hiking shoes; whereas I can't get any traction in these ridiculous riding boots, so I'm slip-sliding across the slush and at constant risk of twisting an ankle.

He doesn't say a word when he realizes I'm not right behind him, just comes back down the path and takes my hand to help me around the most unstable areas. In any other circumstance, this might seem like a chivalrous gesture, but I'm reminded of my mother, who would tug me along at the mall when I was little to keep me from dawdling. I don't care how warm his calloused hands are— there's nothing romantic about them gripping yours so you don't fall on your ass and bruise your tailbone.

After who knows how many minutes, the trees thin out and we come to a clearing. I expect to see his headlamp shining on a quaint log cabin or at least a bare-bones Airbnb, but the only thing I can make out is a large white van.

"Are you going to drive me back? My company's staying at Granite Grove."

His eyes bulge, and a scoff escapes his lips in a foggy exhale. "Not a chance. It's pitch-dark, the road conditions are already not ideal, and out here a small snowstorm can become a blizzard before you know it. We're better off hunkering down tonight, and I can take you back first thing in the morning."

"Hunker down . . . where exactly?" I ask, my head swiveling in search of shelter.

We walk up to the van, and he slaps the side of it. "In my humble abode, of course!"

~

"WHAT YOU CAN LEARN From a Guy's OnlyVans Profile," by The Send-It Sisters on Thursday, January 6

. . .

WE GET IT. You were minding your own business when suddenly you came across a hottie's OnlyVans page. And being the progressive digital citizen you are, you're tempted to support this intriguing #vanlife creator, if only to get a sneak peek of what's under his hood.

But before you impulsively commit to yet another subscription, pay close attention to these four key areas. If you're selective about your sign-ups, you can avoid the van boys and drive home with a new van man.

1. **A picture is worth a thousand groans.** Reviewing bios for red flags is essential, but a profile picture can fill in what's left unsaid between the lines. He may have the eloquence of Shakespeare, but he's no Romeo if his neck has so much beard it looks like it's never seen the sun.

2. **Perks worth every penny.** They say you get what you pay for, so don't cheap out with a lemon. If you want to evolve beyond van-surviving and enjoy van-thriving, pony up for premiums like sustainable energy, meals that don't require a microwave, and a bed big enough to unfurl from the fetal position.

3. **You can't spell GURL without URL.** Vans don't typically come with room for ring lights and tripods, so we don't expect dudes to be camera-ready influencers. But they better have a digital paper trail. So click those links, because a little cyber-snooping can be the difference

between someone being all-American and on *America's Most Wanted*.

4. **Play a little game of "just the tip."** There's no ethical consumption under capitalism, of course, so we believe in supporting creators for their hard work. But if your van vagabond isn't adding more value than the space he's taking up in your driveway, might we suggest the only tip you leave is, "Get a real job."

praise for love on the rocks

"Alyssa Jarrett marries a giggle-and-kick-your-feet romance with tough conversations surrounding mental health and grief, and the result is a book full of heart. *Love on the Rocks* is an utter joy to read."

Jess Land, reviewer at The Romance Report

"Overall, such an enjoyable read. I loved the romance between Nolan and Tania, and her character development in the end is, of course, much appreciated. Perfect happy ending for this impossibly cute couple."

Goodreads reviewer

"Another can't-put-down read by Alyssa Jarrett! A few things I love about her writing—it's funny as hell, so easy to read and enjoy, and she has a way of truly immersing you into the book! *Love on the Rocks* introduces us to a world where rock climbing and van camping intersect with the corporate world. Perfect for rom-com lovers, indie fans, or poolside/vacation reading!"

Goodreads reviewer

about the author

Alyssa Jarrett is a romance author and tech marketer based in the San Francisco Bay Area. When she's not telling steamy, satirical love stories, she can be found drinking an iced tea or cuddling with her cats.

You can subscribe to her newsletter, Grumpy + Sunshine, on Substack, and follow her @authoralyssajarrett on Instagram, Threads, and TikTok.

alyssajarrett.com
alyssajarrett.substack.com

Follow Alyssa online: